KNOCKED OUT BY LOVE

A Love to the Extreme Novel

ABBY NILES

Entangled Publishing, LLC
2614 South Timberline Road
Suite 109
Fort Collins, CO 80525
Visit our website at www.entangledpublishing.com.

Select Contemporary is an imprint of Entangled Publishing, LLC.

Edited by Robin Haseltine and Liz Pelletier
Cover design by LJ Anderson
Cover art from DepositPhotos

Manufactured in the United States of America

First Edition August 2016

To all the readers who fell in love with Brody in Fighting Love *and made his story possible. Thank you.*

Chapter One

Brody "The Iron" Minton leaned one elbow against the polished wood of the outside bar and watched the beach performers dance to the unique beat of steel drums. This was the first time he'd been able to capture some peace and quiet since he'd arrived at the resort six hours ago. He was going to have to steal a lot more of these moments, or he wasn't going to make it through the next week.

"Impressive," his cousin Blake muttered as he motioned with his beer bottle toward the large flame erupting from a young man's mouth, brightening the humid summer air.

"Definitely." Hell, the whole damn place was impressive.

Too bad his youngest sister had about driven him batshit crazy with her fretting, and he hadn't been able to enjoy any of the perks the resort had to offer yet. He wasn't grasping her crazy right now.

It wasn't like her soon-to-be millionaire husband wasn't forking out the big bucks for the lavish destination wedding, including a top-of-the-line event planner to worry about all this shit so his sister wouldn't have to. But his sibling couldn't relax and just enjoy what was supposed to be one of the biggest days of her life. Nope, she had to have herself involved in every damn detail and, in the process, drive everyone else fucking nuts.

Oh well. He hadn't paid a dime for this trip, so she could be as psychotic as she wanted. As long as he stayed off her warpath, he'd enjoy himself. Fuck knew he needed some downtime.

Things with his coach had been going south for a while now. He needed to think about what his next move was going to be when he got back home.

Taking a swig of his beer, he eyed his cousin. Blake was the only other member of his family to join the MMA circuit. Their moms had been close sisters, so he and Blake had spent a lot of time together growing up, which included training as they got into their later teens. As they got older, they went their separate ways, but had always kept in touch. Blake had recently moved back to Atlanta to help his mom out after his father died, and had joined Mike's facility—one of the best MMA gyms in the industry.

"How are things over with Mike?"

Blake shrugged. "He's a moody son-of-a-bitch."

So he'd heard, but the man's reputation spoke for itself. His gym housed two title holders in the biggest MMA circuit around, Cage Match Championship—CMC. Dante "Inferno" Jones was the reigning welterweight champion and Tommy "Lightning" Sparks was the light heavyweight.

"What about you?" Blake asked.

"Not bad."

As much as he'd love to share the shit he was dealing with, he wouldn't. The fighting industry was too small. Not that he thought his cousin would run off at the mouth, but one word in the locker room would spread like wildfire and take on a life of its own. He wasn't ready for all that.

"Word has it Greg's got himself a new game changer on his roster."

Brody tightened his grip on the bottle. The new "game changer" was exactly why he was forced to contemplate his future with the industry. "Yeah. Randy Boss."

"Heavyweight, right?"

"Yep." Brody took a swig of his beer.

"That causing any friction for you, being heavyweight yourself?"

Of course it fucking was. "Not at all. The kid doesn't hold a goddamn candle to me."

Blake smiled and saluted him with his beer bottle. They turned their attention back to the performance. At least he could still talk a convincing game to his cousin. Two heavyweight fighters in the same house shouldn't be a big deal—in theory.

In reality, it was a huge pain in his ass. Since that cocky little prick had waltzed into the facility with Greg fawning over him like some kind of love-struck dolt, Brody's training had gone to complete shit.

Yeah, the kid had an impressive record. Sure, he seemed untouchable, the next Dante "Inferno" Jones of the heavyweight division. And Greg was over the moon at having him in his gym. At finally having a shot at a belt. Talk about a kick-in-the-balls moment—he'd nearly seen stars.

So he wasn't a spring chicken anymore. Thirty wasn't anything to sneeze at, especially in the heavyweight division. The reigning champ was thirty-four. But Randy's age was why he was such a hot commodity to Greg. A young heavyweight with a damn good record meant Greg would get a lot more wear out of him.

Blake turned to him. "Have you been slotted for your next fight?"

Brody's stomach clenched as he took a measured swig off

his beer. Not a topic he really cared to discuss. "Yeah."

When he failed to elaborate, his cousin drawled, "And?"

"Jack Raster."

Blake's head jerked back, and his eyebrows drew together in confusion. "Raster? Why?"

Brody shrugged.

"Dude, I'd be pissed." His cousin cast him a long glance. "Aren't you pissed? That's a fucking downgrade, cuz."

"It's what they offered me."

Though it felt like having scraps tossed at him.

"But you just fought Mitch Colten four months ago and won, man. You shouldn't be wasting your time with fighters who have a mediocre record at best."

"I barely beat Mitch. Remember the headlines?"

Blake grimaced. "Those fucking reporters don't know a goddamn thing. None of them have faced off with another fighter in the cage. It's pure bullshit to call that win pure luck."

But it had been. Even Brody knew it.

Mitch had dominated him in the cage until Brody, bloody and barely keeping to his feet, had gotten lucky in the third round with strong jab on the sweet spot. Blake was being nice about the headlines, not mentioning the articles that had questioned if Brody was at the end of his career. They'd even gone as far as to say he was washed up. It wasn't long after that Greg had brought in Randy and started completely ignoring Brody.

It just added to his doubts about his career. His last two fights hadn't been easy by any means. Maybe it was time for him to retire. Better to do it on a high note instead of being one of those fighters who stayed in past their prime.

Or maybe he needed a change, a new coach. Someone who trained differently. Maybe it would get him out of this lull.

That was the big question he needed to mull over this

week. Did he really want to stay in Atlanta, or get a fresh start somewhere else?

As he brought the bottle up to his lips, he scanned the outside patio and his eyes landed on a blonde wearing a blue and white tie-dyed dress that molded to her curves. A knock hit him in the chest as the lady smiled coyly up at a light-haired gentleman and then took a sip of her drink.

Scoffing at his reaction, he forced his eyes to move on. That hadn't been the first time he'd caught a glimpse of a woman who reminded him of Scarlett. Though it surprised him that this one caught his glance. The woman's hair was much lighter and shorter, and the dress was tighter and more revealing than she tended to wear.

Not even a fucking ocean between Scarlett and him made a difference—he was still always hoping to catch a glimpse of her. Pathetic. And yet another reason why he needed to leave Atlanta.

Coveting his best friend's wife was sick on so many levels.

Then a familiar titter reached his ears, and he stiffened. Slowly, he returned his gaze to the corner. The woman had shifted her position, giving him a clear frontal view of way too much tanned legs and cleavage. His hand tightened on the bottle. The reason the woman reminded him of Scarlett was because she *was* Scarlett—just a spruced up one.

And that Scarlett was not smiling flirtatiously at her husband.

Instinct said to bolt over and intervene. The example of his parents' thirty-seven years of marriage told him not to jump to conclusions. Right now, she wasn't doing anything wrong. Ryan could be in the bathroom, and she was enjoying having a guy show her some interest. That wasn't cheating.

Scarlett laughed at something the man said and laid her left hand on his forearm. Brody's gaze zeroed in on the third finger—the third *ringless* finger, missing its two-karat diamond encrusted gold wedding ring.

How would he notice that? He'd used that goddamn ring as a constant reminder to keep his hands off her.

What the fuck was she doing? Where the hell was Ryan?

"Excuse me," he mumbled to his cousin as he stormed in her direction. She never once took her eyes off the man she was prowling.

That was the only way to interpret her actions. How could she do this to Ryan? The man lived and breathed for her.

As he sidled up beside her, he said, "Hello, Scarlett."

When she turned her head, he expected to see surprise and then instant panic and guilt. Surprise he got in the widening of her blue eyes, but panic and guilt were nowhere to be seen.

"Brody!" She grimaced, rubbed her forehead and muttered a curse under her breath. "So *this* is the resort where Tessa's getting married."

So she knew about the wedding, which meant Ryan had mentioned it to her. But she didn't seem happy about Brody's presence.

"Were you hoping it was a different one?" he asked flatly, with a scathing glare at the other man, who shuffled back a space.

"I was, actually."

Because Ryan had made the plans and conveniently booked a romantic trip at the same resort where his best friend would be staying? That sounded like something Ryan would do, but the lack of a wedding band still didn't fit.

"Where's your *husband*?" He put emphasis on the last word to get the jerk-off beside her to back up.

And it worked.

"Husband?" the other man asked and then held up his hands. "I'm not looking for drama. Sorry. Nice talking to you."

With that, he turned and walked away.

Scarlett whirled on him. "Mind your own damn business, Brody!"

"Where's Ryan, Scarlett?"

She crossed her arms tight across her chest and leveled a defiant glare at him, lips pressed tight.

"He's not here, is he?"

An annoyed brow arched midway up her forehead as her mouth pursed even tighter. Who the hell was this woman? Certainly not the one he thought he knew.

"You picked the wrong resort, huh? Now I'm here, and you can't do what you planned, right?"

Again she said nothing, just continued to stare at him with the same angry expression. What the fuck?

"I'm not going to stand back and watch you cheat on my best friend. I don't work that way."

"Bros before hos, right?" Lowering her arms, she let a nasty snarl curl her lip, taking Brody aback. Everything about this was the opposite of the Scarlett he knew.

"Jesus. What's gotten into you?"

"Nothing yet, but I'm searching for it."

The crass innuendo stunned him speechless. Scarlett *never* acted like this. She was proper to the point of being a prude sometimes. Not that it had ever really bothered him. The way she would blush whenever someone said something risqué had always been so endearing to him.

"You took vows. I thought those meant something to you. You can't cheat on Ryan."

"I can't cheat on Ryan?" She stared at him for a long moment, hands on her hips, then she closed the distance between them until she was right under his nose, looking straight up into his eyes. "Watch me."

Chapter Two

Scarlett shoved open the door to her room and felt a second of satisfaction as it banged against the wall. Her best friend Delaney charged in after her, slamming it closed with as much force as Scarlett had opened it.

"What the hell *happened*?" her friend demanded for the twentieth time since she'd been on her way back from the bathroom and seen Scarlett storm out of the themed beach party.

Scarlett loved Delaney, but talking was the last thing she wanted to do at the moment. She wanted to throw something, rage, and have a completely justifiable meltdown.

Alone. No witnesses. Just her and her pent-up emotions.

Damn it, she was entitled to one after everything she'd been through, and Brody and his judgmental comments made the need all the more gripping.

You took vows.

Screw you, asshole.

"Hey," Delaney said in a soft voice as she laid a hand on Scarlett's shoulder. "Who's got you this upset?"

She shook off her friend's touch.

Why here? She'd known Brody's sister was getting married this weekend somewhere in the Bahamas, but this wasn't the only highly rated all-inclusive resort. There were many of them. So freaking many of them.

"I don't want to talk about it. I'd really like to be alone, if you don't mind."

A soft scoff sounded behind her. "Not happening. You weren't this angry when you found out that louse of a husband of yours was cheating on you. I'm not leaving you to destroy this room. Now spill it."

Because his cheating hadn't been the worst of his sins against her. There'd been so much more. Years of "more." The cheating had simply freed her from trying to save her marriage. That's what she'd been doing when she planned this romantic Caribbean trip. Instead, she'd found the irrefutable proof of his infidelity.

Scarlett stared out the sliding glass doors at nothing, and laid her palm to her lower belly.

A positive pregnancy test. The bitch had been in *her* home. Had taken the test in *her* bathroom. Ryan had been too stupid to cover his tracks.

Who the hell did Brody think he was? He wasn't her keeper. He wasn't the guardian of *her* marriage. He had no right to interfere with her healing. She itched to grab something, hurl it. She fisted her hands to resist the urge.

Delaney was right. She needed to talk before she did something stupid. Inhaling deeply, she turned around. "Brody's here."

Six feet four inches, two-hundred and forty some odd pounds of disapproving man. Just what she needed.

A slight widening of her eyes was the only indication Delaney was surprised. "And he saw you talking to a guy."

Scarlett gave a sardonic laugh. Well, Delaney had put two

and two together pretty fast. Not surprising. Her friend had always been rather intuitive. "You know what Brody had the nerve to say to me after he ran the guy off?"

"I can only imagine."

"He wanted to know how I could do this to Ryan. Said that I couldn't cheat on his best friend."

Delaney grimaced. "Ouch."

"It infuriated me so badly I told him to watch me."

A spurt of laughter came from her friend. "Well that's one way to put him in his place." A serious expression stole over her face as she crossed her arms. "You have to see this from his perspective, though, hon. From his side, I'm sure it didn't look good."

Deep down, she knew she would've jumped to the same conclusion Brody had. Deep down, she knew his reaction wasn't uncalled for. But that was *deep down*.

Raging on the surface was the insult of him questioning *her* fidelity to her husband when he had been the one who'd gotten a piece of ass on the side.

"I really don't care how it looked. In fact, I hope he calls Ryan and tells him I'm down here sleeping with men left and right." Her voice cracked, and she clamped her mouth closed because she couldn't voice the rest. It was too humiliating.

I hope that sorry piece of shit understands that other men find me attractive and exciting in bed.

What kind of karma had she put out in the universe to be rewarded with Brody's presence in a time she needed to be away from everything back home?

She deserved this time to herself. *She'd* done everything right. She'd fought for her marriage, even at her unhappiest, because that was what a married couple was supposed to do. Fight for each other.

Now *she* was feeling like she had to explain herself? To hell with that. She was here to take back some of the happiness

Ryan had stolen from her over the last couple of years.

The first thing she and Delaney had done after checking in was hit the salon. Scarlett needed to update her appearance. It wasn't that she'd let herself go, really, but she hadn't tried very hard, either. The more bad news they'd received, the more distant Ryan had become. Or worse, the more he criticized her in a way she worried she'd never truly bounce back from.

Now honey-colored strands, with some shocking lighter streaks, brushed her shoulders in a sexy layered bob. The cut had taken years off her face. Before, she had felt every one of her twenty-seven years, plus a few additional ones. Now she could easily pass for early to mid-twenties, and she felt good for the first time in a long while.

The blue-and-white silk dress with a hi-lo skirt showed off more leg than she was accustomed to, while the halter-top gave "bada boom" a whole new meaning. Not that she hadn't needed some liquid courage before even leaving the room, and a bit more once men started approaching her.

As the liquor warmed her insides, her tension eased, her worry over what to say abated, and she'd relished the attention, reminding herself that she had all the control. Tonight had been *her* moment. And Brody had ruined it by bringing her ex-husband into her paradise.

"Maybe you should tell Brody everything so he'll leave you alone," Delaney said, thankfully saving Scarlett from her thoughts.

"I don't owe him an explanation."

He could take his overly muscled ass straight to hell for all she cared.

She sighed in resignation. "You're absolutely right. You don't."

Though she owed him nothing, she wasn't ready to rehash the events leading up to her escape. The only person who knew even the smallest portion about what had happened was Delaney. She wanted to keep it that way.

Soon enough, she would have to face the music of her failed marriage. She was dreading dealing with her mother and sister. Everyone loved Ryan and had refused to entertain the idea that he was cheating. Instead, they sided with him, saying she was in a bad place mentally, and it was making her suspicious over everything and everybody.

How wrong they'd been.

How would they react when they found out she'd been right? Would they see the snake Ryan was behind his easy smile and adoring facade, or would they blame her suspicions for causing him to stray? She wished she could be confident her family would support her, but they hadn't in the past when it came to Ryan, so she wasn't sure they would now.

Maybe it was selfish of her to want to stick her head in the sand while she was here, but she'd been living in a harsh reality for far too long, and it was past time she got a chance to just live.

"So if you're not going to explain anything to Brody, what are you going to do to get him to lay off?" Delaney asked.

"Nothing." She raised her hands in a helpless gesture at Delaney's confused look. "What am I supposed to do? If he wants to have double standards, that's on him. I don't have to play along."

"Double standards?"

"Come on. There's no way he doesn't know what Ryan's been doing. If he wants to judge me for cheating while he *knows* his boy is doing the same damn thing, then I'm going to give him an eyeful to go back and tattle to Ryan about."

"He might not know, Scar. We all have secrets and I didn't tell you everything about my relationship."

"Why wouldn't you?"

Stupid question. It was the same reason she wasn't telling Delaney everything about Ryan. Delaney's ex-boyfriend had been a real piece of work. There had been many times where Delaney had said to Scarlett, "I am not this woman. Why am I being this woman?"

Love made you stupid, that's why.

God knew she'd lost a few IQ points, even with her gut screaming at her something was wrong. In the beginning, she'd clung to any excuse Ryan had given her, refusing to believe he would lie. It was hard to admit how foolish she'd been, even to her best friend.

"Because I knew how you'd react, and I didn't want to hear it. It's as simple as that." She shrugged. "So, as far as I'm concerned, the jury is still out on whether Brody is guilty of being in the know."

"My jury isn't. He used to hang around our place at least four days a week. I considered him my friend, too, not just my husband's. But a little over a year ago, he stopped coming over. Ryan still hangs with him a few times a week, but I'm never invited."

She'd been surprised at how much it had hurt to have Brody cut her off like he had. She'd looked forward to his visits, and there had been plenty of times Brody had swooped in to take her to dinner or a movie when Ryan had been unavailable or just plain unwilling to go. At least now she knew the reason for his retreat—he had been protecting his bro.

"Maybe Brody was a cover so Ryan could see his girlfriend."

She ran her fingers through her hair. "The timeline is there. Ryan starts seeing a woman on the side, his best friend stops hanging around the house. Can't be any clearer than that."

Delaney scrunched her nose. "Yeah. It does seem pretty clear. So what are you going to do?"

All she was looking for was a little male attention to stroke her ego. She needed it. So did Delaney. Both of them had decided to use this trip to learn to flirt again and slide back into single life. Neither one of them was looking for a hookup, but Brody didn't need to know that.

"Screw Brody. He's not going to ruin my good time." She strode across the room and opened the door, then glanced over her shoulder. "Project 'Watch Me' is officially underway."

• • •

"Damn it," Brody muttered between clenched teeth, and fisted his hand around his cell phone as he paced the palm-lined walkway. The calming sound of the ocean waves crashing in the background had no effect on his disgust at himself.

For the last hour, he'd been struggling to do his duty to his best friend. What a shitty friend that made him out to be. Had the shoe been on the other foot, he would be furious with Ryan if he hadn't informed him that his hypothetical wife was waltzing around without her wedding band on, flirting with men—much less insinuating her intention of finding a man to *get into her*.

So why the hell was he hesitating?

He sighed. Because there had to be more to the story. There were women out there, married and single, who were born flirters, who could captivate any man they came across without even trying. Scarlett wasn't one of those women.

Unless she was in front of her students, she was very introverted. She also exuded an inaccessibility that kept most men from approaching her. The ones who attempted to engage her in conversation would receive a bored, "go waste someone else's time" stare. The Scarlett he'd just seen was completely out of character, which meant something had to be motivating her.

What could have happened? Had she and Ryan fought? He shook off that possibility. A fight wouldn't cause this drastic of a personality change.

He gritted his teeth and shoved his phone back in his pocket. The best course of action was to keep watch over her and not bring Ryan into it until he knew exactly what the fuck was going on with her.

"Where in the hell did you go, man?" Brody turned to find Blake walking up the path toward him. "I turned around to watch the show for a second, then when I glanced back, you were just gone," his cousin continued.

"Sorry about that. I saw someone I knew."

"Who?"

"You wouldn't know her. She's Ryan's wife."

"So, he's here?" his cousin asked, his lips pressing together tightly.

"What do you have against him?" Brody had never understood Blake's obvious distaste for Ryan.

"Let's just say Ryan and I have never meshed well, and leave it at that."

Considering the only time they'd spent any real time together had been when they were teens, Brody blew off his dislike as some juvenile rivalry.

"It doesn't matter. He's not here. Just his wife."

"Some sort of girl's weekend?"

He hoped so. This would be even more fucked up if she were here alone. "Not sure. I only saw her."

Two women passing behind Blake in the distance caught Brody's attention. The tight, tie-dyed dress helped him recognize one of them immediately, and the noticeably inebriated sway of her walk concerned him. Scarlett wasn't a drinker, but it was damn clear she was drunk as hell, especially as she tripped over her own feet and started giggling. Yet another out of character moment. But at least it looked like she wasn't here alone.

"Let's see where those two end up," Brody said, nudging

his chin in the ladies' direction.

Blake glanced over his shoulder and whistled softly. "I like the way you think, cousin. That one in the blue dress... *daaaamn*."

Brody scowled. "She's off-limits."

Blake turned back toward him and raised a brow. "Calling dibs?"

"Yeah, I'm calling dibs. She's Ryan's wife."

He had to keep repeating those words to remind himself. He wasn't sure what she was up to, but the lack of a wedding band was way more tempting than he wanted to admit. No matter if she had a ring or not, she would *always* be his best friend's wife.

"Seriously, dude?" Blake jerked his head back in surprise. "You going stalker?"

"No. But I'm here, and Ryan isn't. If she's up to something, I need to know."

"I think it's her business, and whatever's going on inside her marriage is none of yours."

Truer words had never been spoken. So why did he feel like he had to get to the bottom of it? Why did it seem so damn important?

He really couldn't take the time to analyze it. He'd spent most of the last two years—especially the last year—doing anything *but* analyzing the way he did or didn't feel about Scarlett.

"Maybe so," he said. "But either way, if I know she's just having a fun girl's weekend, then I can go about my own business. If it's not, I really need to let Ryan know."

Blake studied him for a long minute. "All right, cuz. You do what you got to do. The dark-haired one in the black dress is a lot shorter than I usually go for, but definitely smokin'."

"That's Delaney, Scarlett's best friend. Don't let her size fool you. She might be barely five feet, but she's feisty as hell."

"Not married, right? I have no interest in getting caught up in any drama."

"Last time I saw her, she was in a relationship with some dude Scarlett didn't like, but that was almost a year ago."

"Relationships are fair game, my man. I don't fuck with married women, but if a guy isn't smart enough to claim one, then she's still on the market." Blake winked then turned in the direction the girls had gone.

Brody kept his distance. The way Scarlett had reacted earlier when he'd confronted her, she would flip the hell out if she saw him openly following her. He didn't want or need that. He just wanted to watch her, make sure she was really okay. *Damn it.* He didn't like how drunk she was. Alcohol mixed with her earlier attitude was a fucking recipe for disaster. Hell, he didn't know much about Delaney. Was it possible she'd given Scarlett something stronger than alcohol?

When the girls entered one of the resort's bars, thumping eighties music poured out the door. Blake halted with a grimace. "Not my scene, dude."

It wasn't Brody's, either. In Atlanta, there was a popular club called the Boot Scoot that most of the fighters frequented. He was not one of them, and only went a couple of times a year to be social with the guys at his gym. Clubs had never been his thing. Too loud, too crowded, and too full of drunk people. However, for Scarlett he was willing to make an exception.

"We're on vacation. Might as well broaden our horizons."

Blake muttered under his breath as he stalked to the door and yanked it open. As the music blasted him, his irritated scowl contorted to mock pain, but he stepped inside anyway. Brody followed, wincing at the volume.

"I can't even fucking think in here," Blake yelled over Kenny Loggins's "Footloose."

At least the music wasn't techno. He could deal with

throwbacks. He glanced around the inside, which was decorated with 80s memorabilia, ranging from posters of the Brat Pack to hair bands. Though the overhead lights were dimmed, the four bouncing spotlights positioned in each corner brightened the place. While there was a sizable attendance, there was also adequate breathing room.

Thank God. One thing that sucked more than being in a club was being in a packed, dark one.

Someone jostled him from behind and he sighed. So much for breathing room. The drunks were out in full force. Another reason he hated the bar scene. He got knocked around enough during training and in the cage. He liked space outside of his career. "Let's find a place not so in the middle of the crowd."

As he wove his way around the idiots standing smack in front of the doorway, making for a side wall, he searched for Scarlett, but couldn't locate her. This wasn't her scene, either. Had she realized that and slipped out when he wasn't looking?

After he got situated against the wall, he scanned over the gyrating bodies on the dance floor and finally spotted her about thirty feet away, standing with her back to him at a small round table on the adjacent wall, laughing with Delaney.

That was innocent enough.

Maybe he'd just pissed her off earlier by insinuating she was doing something wrong. Maybe she'd simply taken her wedding ring off to put on lotion and forgotten to put it back on. Hell, maybe she hadn't had the ring for a while—the damn thing could've fallen down the sink or something. All these were more probable than something being up with Ryan and Scarlett's marriage.

A surprising amount of disappointment settled over him, and he cursed the feeling to hell and back. Damn if that didn't say something about the kind of friend he was. He should feel relief for Ryan and guilt for accusing Scarlett, but his first emotion was purely selfish. The most sickening thing was it wouldn't matter if they were having problems. He could never have Scarlett—married, divorced, or heaven forbid, widowed. She would always be the wife of his best friend. That would never change.

"You know what?" he said to his cousin. "This is stupid. Let's get out of here."

"You sure?"

"Yeah. I saw some pool tables in one of the lounges. Want to…" His voice trailed off as a blond-haired man who looked like he stepped off the cover of *Playgirl* approached the two women.

Blake heaved a sigh, leaned back against the wall, and crossed his arms.

As much as Brody wanted to leave, wanted to believe his own rationalizations, he couldn't get his legs to move toward the door. He silently encouraged the man to focus on Delaney, but his charming smile stayed glued on Scarlett, who had shifted to face the guy. Brody no longer saw her back, but had a clear side view. Unlike the numerous times in the past he'd watched a man get shot down by a single glare from her, this time she was encouraging, while also being flirtatiously coy.

Though he couldn't hear her over the music, he saw her lips part wide in one of her truly amused laughs. The pleased, almost cocky expression on the guy's face only confirmed it. She stepped closer to him and pressed her body into his. He lowered his hand to the curve of her hip, much lower than was appropriate for a happily married woman. She toyed with the collar of his shirt then ran her finger down his chest, bottom lip tucked seductively between her teeth.

Who the hell was this woman?

Then out of nowhere, she cupped the man's face between her palms and kissed him square on the lips—slow, encouraging, a kiss that flat out said, "If you want it, take it."

The dude wasted no time in sliding both arms around her waist, pulling her closer and deepening the kiss. A clear "fuck yeah, I want it," if Brody ever saw one.

A red haze of fury obstructed his vision as he watched her melt into the other man. He'd like to believe it was only indignation over her betrayal of his best friend, but it wasn't. He'd never liked watching her kiss her husband, either—one of the reasons he'd put so much distance between Scarlett and him this past year.

She pulled back from the kiss but stayed pressed tightly against him, lifted up on her tiptoes, and whispered something into his ear. Her glazed eyes, bright from drink and not passion, stared up at the guy as she waited for his response. He gave an eager nod. Smiling brightly, she stepped back, took his hand, then stumbled a little to the left before catching herself on some random woman standing behind her.

Delaney uncertainly laid a hand on Scarlett's forearm and said something at which Scarlett laughed and shook her head. Delaney pressed her lips together tightly, worry evident in the glance she cast the guy.

As the man snaked his arm around Scarlett's waist to lead her toward the exit, she went without a second of hesitation. Delaney, however, hurried in front of the pair. She exuded nothing but fierce disapproval, so it didn't take a genius to figure out she was trying to talk some damn sense into her drunk friend.

At least one of them seemed to have some.

In response, Scarlett wrapped herself around the man, and his shit-eating grin made it clear that she'd been told to move. Delaney shook her head sharply and planted her hands on her hips.

"That don't look too good," Blake muttered.

Brody agreed, but he stayed where he was, waiting to see if Delaney would be able to handle the situation on her own.

He would rather not interfere again. He'd already pissed off Scarlett in a way he'd never seen before, and he really didn't want to egg her on in her current condition. God only knew what the fuck she would do as drunk as she was, when she'd seemed willing to do practically anything sober.

He sure as hell wouldn't be the reason she went over the edge and did something she couldn't take back.

"You going to intervene here, cuz?" Blake asked as the standoff between the threesome stretched on.

He shook his head slightly, keeping his gaze locked on Delaney, whose posture shouted: *Do not leave with him.*

Finally, Delaney locked her fingers around her friend's forearm and tugged. Scarlett yanked away, scowling. The man tried to usher her around the other woman again, but she shuffled in front of them. An awkward dance ensued, and all the while, the tiny woman's fierce you-will-not-leave-with-my-drunk-friend-asshole expression never slipped.

"You're right. She's a feisty little thing," Blake said, his words tinged with awe, which was a huge thing coming from him. Other people rarely impressed him.

"Delaney has never taken shit from anyone."

She was proving that more than ever, and her protector stance was obviously starting to get under Scarlett's skin. She let go of the man and swayed close to her friend, finger raised, anger pulling her lips tight to slightly bare her teeth.

What the fuck?

Brody's brows pulled together. Scarlett wasn't a saint. She did get angry like every other person on the planet, but her anger had always been displayed with a purse of the lips, clench of the jaw, and jutting up of the chin—and a death stare that went right through you. He would know. He'd had it directed at him once when he'd brought Ryan home from his bachelor party so staggering drunk that he had puked right on the carpet at her bare feet.

But this aggressive woman looking like she'd actually attack her best friend of eighteen years was not Scarlett at all.

The two women exchanged heated words and sharp gesticulations. Then lips did purse, a jaw did clench, and a chin jutted up in the air. But it wasn't Scarlett's. It was Delaney's as she moved aside and swept her arm in a dramatic fashion toward the exit.

Oh. Hell. No.

"You're on, cuz," Blake said. "She's too drunk to be leaving with that fucker."

"Already on it."

Brody rushed toward them. By the widening of Delaney's eyes and the sudden relaxing of her shoulders, she saw his approach. Not that he needed permission to step in, but he wouldn't lie—having her best friend's support would go a long way tomorrow when Scarlett was nursing one hell of a hangover.

Scarlett leaned against the guy as they made their way to the door. Brody picked up the pace and lunged forward to latch his hand around her elbow. "You're not going anywhere."

Scarlett's head snapped down to his fingers then slowly lifted. Fury brightened those blue eyes.

"Let. Go," she bit out between clenched teeth.

Had she really just gritted? Holy fucking shit.

"Nope," he said. "You're staying right here."

The guy stepped forward and tapped-shoved his shoulder with the tips of his fingers. "Hey, buddy. You need to move along."

Brody stared down at the place the man had poked him then lifted his gaze to the fucker. "Touch me again, asshole, and see what happens."

The man paled visibly, swallowed, and took a step back. He still managed to say, "Just leave the lady alone, okay."

"I'm the bad guy? You're trying to escort an intoxicated

woman out of a bar—even though her best friend has been trying to stop you for the last five minutes—and *I'm* the bad guy?"

"I was just going to help her back to her room."

"I'm sure you were, but we no longer need your *help*." He all but sneered the word. "I'll take it from here."

Scarlett jerked her arm out of his grip. "The hell. I'm goin' with 'im."

The guy smirked and started to put his arm around her waist again.

"Touch her and I'll break your face," Brody said with every bit of the cage fighter he had in him.

The man was smart enough to lower his arm. A huff came from Scarlett, and she swayed forward and poked him hard in the chest.

"Mindyerbusiness," she slurred through the reek of alcohol. "My life. My party."

Goddamn, how much had she had to drink?

"Wait," the guy said. "You know him?"

"Course, I know 'im. 'E's Brody 'Leavemethefuckalone' Minton."

The guy's eyes widened as his gaze raked Brody up and down. "Holy shit."

"Yeah. Tell all your other buddies that Brody '*The Iron*' Minton says this woman is off-limits or they'll deal with me."

"Yeah. No problem." He started backing away slowly, and Scarlett's eyes bulged almost comically.

"Don't be a wuss. 'E's not gonna do anythin'." She slashed her arm toward Brody. "'E's like a fuckin' kitty cat. Never even hit nothin' outside of the stupid cage. Hell, 'e even owns a kitty cat named Princess." She chortled.

What she said was true, but she underestimated him. He would hit that man and any other fucker who messed with her. "Don't test me, Scarlett."

The man kept backing away.

She actually stomped her foot. "Don't go!"

He just waved his arms then turned and bolted.

Scarlett spun on Brody. "You. Suck!"

"Come on. You need to lie down." He took her arm again and started to turn her toward the exit.

Again, she yanked away from him. "I'll lie down when I damn well want to."

She was so volatile. A mass of bubbling rage that was about to explode. Where the hell was all this intensity coming from? Was this the explanation for his best friend's absence? Had Scarlett had some sort of mental meltdown? Ryan hadn't mentioned anything when they'd hung out last week. All his best friend ever talked about was how well their marriage was going and how happy he was.

Scarlett looked far from happy.

"You're starting to make a scene," Delaney said as she stepped up to the two of them.

"I. Don't. Care!" She stumbled back. "I won't go back to my room."

Delaney sent Brody a pleading look. "I can't handle her right now. Honestly, I don't even know what to do. I've never seen her like this."

It was a relief to know he wasn't the only one thinking Scarlett wasn't acting like herself. "Don't worry about it. I've got it. I'll take her back to my room and make sure she doesn't leave."

"Thank you, Brody."

He nodded then stepped toward Scarlett again. She pointed at him. "Stay back. I won't go to my room."

Heat crept up his neck, from embarrassment or anger he wasn't sure. He was feeling both pretty damn hardcore right now. He hated being in the middle of public drama. People were gawking like they were watching a live taping of *Days of our Lives*. And that pissed him off. Not to mention the fact he was completely over Scarlett's antics. Drunk or not, she needed to get her shit together.

The more she backed away from him, the angrier he was getting. Charging her, he grabbed her around the waist and tossed her over his shoulder, not missing a step toward the exit. Thunderous clapping erupted around him, making the moment even more humiliating. God, he couldn't wait to tell Scarlett every goddamn gory detail of this encounter tomorrow so she'd be as mortified as he was.

As he stormed out of the club and made his way down the garden path, he ignored the curious stares from the people he passed. Fuck, he'd stare, too, if there was a man carrying a raving lunatic over his shoulder.

And that was exactly what Scarlett was right now. Raving. Lunatic.

She beat her fists against his lower back, sputtered obscenities, demands, and threats. By the time he shoved his card in the lock and banged open the door to his room, his patience was completely gone. He strode across to the bathroom. After opening the glass door to the walk-in shower, he dropped Scarlett onto the natural-colored marble floor then turned on the shower full blast.

Icy cold water hit her square in the face, and she sputtered then scrambled to get out. He put his hand on top of her head and kept her there. When she tried to wrestle away and crawl between his legs, he stepped over her, ignoring the biting chill of the water as it saturated his shirt to his skin. Crouching, he wrapped his arms around her waist, lifted her up, and sat down with her.

The water beat down on her face and neck, splashing up onto his face. She struggled to get free, raking her nails across his knuckles and bucking against his hold. If he hadn't been so damn furious with her, he would've laughed at her feeble attempts to wiggle free from him. When she apparently realized that he had no intention of letting her go, she screamed—long and loud. He grimaced. Fuck, he hoped no one heard that. The last thing he needed on top of all this was to deal with local authorities.

Suddenly, she went quiet and completely still. He waited for a renewed burst of energy, but she remained silent. Had she passed out?

Just as he had that thought, a weird sound came from her, and her shoulders jerked. He loosened his grip, and her head flopped forward, shoulders still shaking.

"Scarlett?" Fuck, had he hurt her? He leaned around her and fumbled to turn the water off.

As the sounds of the cascading water died, the sad muffled whimper came again. He shifted to her side and gently brushed back the curtain of drenched blond hair. Her teeth clamped down hard on her bottom lip, her chin wobbling.

"Scarlett?"

She slowly looked up at him. Mascara stained the skin under eyes and streaked down her cheeks as tears illuminated the blue of her eyes.

"I just wanted to be wanted," she murmured before the slight control she had over her emotions broke, and she pressed her face into his wet shirt and sobbed.

They were deep, soul-wrenching sobs, the cries of someone who'd been hurt terribly. Unsure of what to do, he kept his arms to his side, but the longer she wept, the more he needed to hold her—to take away whatever pain she was feeling.

He wrapped his arms tight around and let her cry herself out. When she finally grew silent, he asked, "Do you want to talk about it?"

He felt the shake of her head against his chest.

I just wanted to be wanted.

What could she have meant by that? Ryan had told him

just last week how he had taken her on a romantic getaway to the mountains. How they had had such a wonderful time together…

A soft snore reached his ears, and he glanced down. Lips slightly parted, eyes closed—she was more passed out than asleep. He felt for her. She was going to be hurting in the morning.

This presented a bit of a dilemma, though. He couldn't put Scarlett to bed in wet clothes. While stripping this woman had always been a forbidden fantasy of his, her drunken weeping had never played into the picture.

He stood then lifted her in his arms and carried her into the bedroom. After laying her down on the couch, he closed the shutters on the sliding glass doors that overlooked the ocean. He returned to the bathroom and grabbed one of the white terry cloth robes, then came to stand beside the couch.

Looking down at her, he allowed his gaze to follow the soft lines of her face. Even passed out cold from too much alcohol, she looked more like the Scarlett he'd known for years.

Soft. Sweet. Innocent.

The hard woman from before was a mystery to him, a layer of Scarlet he never realize existed. It was too bad it took…whatever had happened…to free this side of her.

Taking a deep breath, he shifted her so he could unzip the back of the dress. He kept his eyes adverted while the fabric fell loose. God knew, he was going to have to look eventually, and there was no need to torture himself sooner than necessary. Once he had the zipper undone, and the top of the dress had slid from her arms, he laid her back down. Keeping his gaze on the dress and not on her skin, he quickly yanked it the rest of the way off and let it plop to the ground.

A lump formed in his throat when he was faced with an undressed Scarlett. The only thing covering her beautiful, sun-kissed skin was a slip of black lace between her legs and a matching bra. Jesus.

He snatched the robe off the arm of the couch and quickly wrapped her in it, knotting the belt at her waist. He carried her to the bed, and after covering her with the blankets, he knew he had to call Ryan.

This was no longer about Scarlett out to cheat on her husband. This was something else entirely. Since Ryan seemed oblivious to it, he needed to let his best friend know what he'd witnessed so he'd be ready for her when she came home.

As he stepped out to the patio then onto the sand, he pulled out his cell phone and pressed the number for his friend. A light breeze blew his hair as he listened to the crash of the waves.

Ryan answered after a couple of rings. "Hello?"

Brody opened his mouth to respond but was interrupted by a feminine voice that caused a rock to form in his stomach.

"It's two o'clock in the morning. Who the hell's calling?"

A scraping noise came through the speaker, sounding very much like a palm being pressed over the phone. Though it dulled Ryan's voice, it didn't mute it. "Shhh. A friend of mine. Go back to sleep." Then in a much louder voice. "Brody? What's up?"

Feeling bitch-slapped, he dropped his arm and stared at his phone. What the fuck? He lifted the cell back to his ear, but he couldn't get one word to pass his stunned mouth. He hung up.

Turning back toward the room, he stared at the woman curled up in his bed, reheard her words, replayed her sobbing.

He'd had it all wrong. She wasn't cheating on her husband. Her husband was cheating on her—and Scarlett knew all about it.

The sudden excitement he felt scared the fucking shit out of him.

Chapter Three

Scarlett's stomach lurched as she rolled over onto her back, groaning. Her mouth felt like a sandstorm had passed through, and she licked her dry tongue across her parched lips, trying to spur on some moisture. The pounding behind her eyes was cruel and unusual punishment.

Kill me now.

She had no one to blame but herself. What had started as a way to relax had spiraled completely out of control.

Prying open her eyes, she flinched away from the bright room, groaning again.

"Here. Drink this."

The deep, masculine voice surprised the crap out of her, and she stiffened as she stared at the ceiling, refusing to look at the unknown man. She tried recollecting a name, a face, but last night was nothing but a big blur.

She hadn't really gone through with bringing a man back to her room, had she? She talked a good game yesterday, but that was all it had been—talk. Oh God, what had she done? Not once in her life had she ever done a one-night stand. She didn't even know the proper etiquette for such a situation. Did she stay for a while to chitchat, or did she get up and leave ASAP?

"Scarlett? Drink this."

Wait. That voice sounded very, very familiar. Turning her head on the pillow, she found Brody towering beside the bed, the same disapproval as yesterday still radiating from his caramel-colored eyes. Refusing to witness his obvious judgement, she lowered her gaze to his broad shoulders then to his red cotton tank. They continued down his muscular arm, taking in the amazing, colorful comic-book themed sleeve, then settled on the orange sports drink in his hand.

Yuck.

She looked past him. Right outside the overly large sliding glass door was the beach. That wasn't her view. What was she doing in Brody's room? She slowly pushed to a sitting position. As the covers fell to her waist, she stilled at the terrycloth robe wrapped around her.

"Where are my clothes?"

"Don't remember anything, huh? Can't say I'm surprised."

She swallowed, panic squeezed her chest. "Did we…I mean…"

Mortifying heat warmed her face. She hated that reaction whenever she tried to talk about sex. It happened every damn time. All she was trying to get out was had they hooked up. And like all the times before, she found herself struggling for words.

"Sleep together?" Brody lifted a brow. "No. I slept on the couch."

She breathed a sigh of relief. "Oh, thank God. Then what happened to my clothes?"

"I hung them outside last night to dry them out."

Scarlett stared at him as she tried to remember why her dress would be wet in the first place. Nothing came to mind.

"Did I jump in the pool or something?"

"That would've been preferable."

Jesus. What *had* she done last night? From the disapproval radiating from Brody, nothing good. "Just tell me. I can't remember anything."

"I tossed you in the shower to shock some sobriety into you. You passed out. I couldn't put you to bed soaking wet."

Well, if that didn't give her a cringe-worthy impression of how bad off she'd been. "How did I end up with you? I know I was with Delaney, and we'd gone to a couple of the bars, but I don't remember bumping into you."

"You didn't really bump into me. I inserted myself into a situation between you, some fucker, and Delaney."

"At one of the bars?"

"Yeah. It's pretty safe to say you won't be easily forgotten by a lot of people around here."

A scene flashed inside her mind. She pressed her hand to her mouth. "Ohmygod. You actually carried me out over your shoulder."

Brody confirmed her words with a tight smile. "Some of that memory coming back?"

She lowered her head into both hands and groaned. "I'm so sorry, Brody."

"Honestly, it's Delaney you probably want to apologize to."

Her head snapped up, and then she immediately wished she hadn't done that, as a slice of pain went through her temple. Rubbing the throb with two fingers, she asked, "What did I do?"

"She was trying to be a good friend to you, and you got pissy about it."

If Delaney was trying to stop her from doing something, then whatever it had been was bad. "I suck."

"I'm not going to argue with that."

Ouch. "You can stop with the holier-than-thou crap. It's clear I screwed up. I'm human. It happens."

"You're right." He took a deep inhale and released it in one huge rush. "I apologize."

She'd known Brody a long time. Something was bothering him. He was stiff, snarky, and uncomfortable. Had she said something last night about the state of her marriage? There was a good chance she had, and God only knew what confessions had spewed from her drunken mouth. She felt heat warm her skin again. To distract herself, she took a sip of the sports drink and winced at its strong orange flavor. She abhorred sports drinks, but knew she was dehydrated and needed the electrolytes. Brody stood staring at her intensely. Avoiding his gaze, she looked around his room—a much larger and nicer room than hers.

On her budget, she couldn't afford one of the rooms that opened right on the beach like this one did. Their room was located on the third floor, and was a good distance from the ocean. The view was still beautiful, but nothing like the one a few feet away through the floor-to-ceiling sliding glass door.

"This had to cost a small fortune," she said, trying to steer the topic away from last night.

"Yeah. Most likely."

"You don't know for sure?"

"Didn't pay for it. Tessa's fiancé did. He paid for the entire trip."

That got her to look back at him and his intense stare. "Wow. You've got a *huge* family. Who's she marrying? Donald Trump?"

"Something like that. I've only met the guy a few times, with her living in New York now."

"How'd they meet?"

"According to Tess, it was a classic Cinderella story. She was falling flat on her face in New York and needed some extra money. She started cleaning apartments on the side. He's a job she landed, and, well…she went from scrubbing floors to riding in limos."

Poor Tessa. She was so wrapped up in the fantasy of it all. One day, though, reality would seep into the relationship, and that was when love was really tested.

"I hope her fairy tale doesn't end," she muttered.

"What was that?" Brody asked.

"Nothing."

Silence stretched between them, then a heavy sigh came from Brody's direction. "Scarlett, I've known you for a long time. Even before you got completely shit-faced last night, you were acting weird, like someone not you at all."

She glanced away. "Maybe I wanted to be someone different."

"Why?"

"What do you mean why? Don't people do that all the time? Hell, don't *you* do that every time you step inside the cage? I happen to know for a fact the fighter isn't the same man I used to sit around and chat superhero movies with."

"Okay, fine," he said between clenched teeth. "I was trying to let you do this on your own, but I guess you're going to make me the douche and just come out and slap you with it."

"Slap me with what?"

"Your behavior concerned me last night, so I called Ryan."

Her entire world stilled. "You called Ryan." She swallowed. "And what did he say?"

A wave of humiliation surged through her. She cursed it. She had nothing to be embarrassed about, nothing to be ashamed of. *She* had done everything right. Those reminders didn't help. All she could think about was Ryan telling Brody how disappointing she was in bed, how he had to go outside their marriage to find a woman who could actually please him. Things he had most likely already told the fighter, but having them reiterated when she'd been at her weakest was mortifying.

"He didn't say anything. I hung up."

She blinked. "Why?"

"Because I got my answer without having to talk to him."

It took her a second to follow his words. A gust of air shot from her mouth.

Brody hadn't known. Ryan had never shared his dirty little secret with his best friend. To confirm this, she asked, "She was there, wasn't she?"

He sucked on his teeth for a second, before he gave an awkward nod. "Yeah. Asked from the background who was calling so late." He paused before saying, "Scarlett, I didn't know."

It would've been easier on her if he had. At least then she could be angry at him. Now she couldn't be. "I often wondered if he was really with you when he claimed to be. You used to hang out at our place all the time, but over the last year you stopped coming around, and when he started going to your place...I was rarely included."

A slight grimace crossed his face, which she didn't understand. "I can't say that every time Ryan said he was with me he was, but we still did hang out a lot. I just got busy, and he was busy, so it got easier to hang out at my place or meet at a restaurant and have a few drinks to catch up."

"I guess there's a small comfort that not *every* word that came out of the bastard's mouth was a lie."

"How long has it been going on?"

She shrugged. "I don't know for sure."

"When did you find out?"

"A few days ago."

The last thing she'd said to the asshole before she'd gone

to stay with Delaney was they were over, and she was filing for divorce. The relief on his face had one clear meaning—he wanted the divorce as much as she did. She'd gone to a lawyer and started the process the very next day.

"Well, that makes things a lot clearer." He shook his head, muttering a curse. "Ryan's an idiot, Scarlett."

She rubbed her forehead. This was not a discussion she was comfortable having with Brody. "It is what it is, right?"

She could now move on without any *what ifs*.

Except one big one. That *what if* didn't apply to her marriage falling apart, but it could keep her from completely letting go of the past—what if she got involved with another man and was just as disappointing to him in bed as she'd been to Ryan? What if she became the woman all men cheated on because she was lousy in the bedroom?

She hated herself for even thinking that about herself. But over the last couple of years, as things between them had gotten edgier, Ryan had started to constantly critique her lovemaking—made it clear he was bored with their intimate time and she had to loosen up to spice it up. The added stress had only made her tense up more. As it was, they hadn't had sex in eight months. Though, his girlfriend probably had a lot to do with that. Still didn't change the fact he'd sought someone else to please him in the bedroom because she was apparently lousy at it.

"What, exactly, was the point of this trip?" Brody asked.

How did she respond to that? Hell, how did she *want* to respond to that?

"I wanted to get reacquainted with the single me." When his eyes narrowed, she quickly added, "It's been a long time since I've been single, Brody. Ryan and I have been together almost eight years. I didn't keep my flirting skills warmed up during our marriage, not like he apparently had, so I'm rusty."

"Scarlett." He raked a hand down his face. "Do you have

any clue that you were going to allow some strange man to escort you back to your room last night?"

No. She didn't remember that.

"Listen," he continued. "If you want to flirt some, then go for it, but for God's sake, be safe about it, and leave the liquor out of the equation."

She bit her lip. That had been a very foolish, rookie mistake that could've had terrible consequences. The only reason she'd drunk the way she had last night was because she'd needed the liquid courage. Unfortunately, she'd drunk way too much of it.

"I was nervous," she admitted hesitantly.

The way Brody's eyes rounded would've been funny if she hadn't been dead serious.

"About talking to guys? You've got nothing to be worried about."

"You're just saying that to make me feel better."

"You're kidding, right? Jesus, Scarlett, you have to know how fucking hot you are."

Flutters erupted in her stomach. No one had called her fucking hot before—not even Ryan. "Now you're going overboard."

He gave her an incredulous look. "You've lost your damn mind."

"Brody, you've known me a long time. When is the last time you saw me in anything outside of teacher clothes or casual jeans and a T-shirt?"

He shrugged. "You're hot as fuck in anything you wear."

Again her stomach fluttered in unexpected excitement at his words. She never thought of herself as hot. Pretty, yes. But when she thought of hot women it was always along the lines of Sofia Vergara—even she thought that woman was hot— and she definitely didn't fall into the same category as the voluptuous Columbian.

Ryan had said she looked beautiful and in the beginning, had thought she looked adorable in pigtails and such. But hot had never been one of the adjectives he'd used to compliment her. She found she liked it—a lot. It made some inner vixen she didn't even know she had perk up and take notice.

"So, you think I'm hot?"

Brody blinked, then swallowed. "I wouldn't have said it if I didn't mean it."

"Would *you* date me?" She was stunned at her own audacity, but the question just popped out.

His gaze slid away toward the patio before returning to hers. "If you weren't my best friend's wife—" Her eyes bulged in protest, and he held up his hands. "Sorry. Ex-wife."

"I know it's not official. I know it's a process, but the moment I found out—"

About the baby.

She inhaled deeply, then released slowly. No. Don't even go there. It was enough he was cheating. That Ryan was going to be a father after their infertility struggles was an agonizing pain she couldn't bear just now. "The moment I found out he was cheating, he ceased being my husband"—she patted over her heart—"here. To me, that's all that matters. I'm no longer his wife in anything but a legal sense, and that'll be easily remedied."

"Divorces takes a while, Scarlett."

"Not if it's uncontested. Since I don't want a damn thing from that sorry piece of shit, other than to take my name back and be legally free of him, we'll have this wrapped up in a few weeks." She waved her hands in frustration. "We've gotten off topic. I don't want to talk about Ryan. You never finished your answer. If I hadn't been married to your jerkface friend, would you date me?"

"In a fucking minute."

"You're not just flattering me?"

"I've always thought Ryan was a lucky son of a bitch. Now I just think he's a stupid one."

"Thank you, Brody."

She wasn't sure how much of what Brody was saying was to make her feel better, but she could honestly say that he had helped. Before he'd stopped coming around, he'd done that a lot. If she was in the dumps and Brody showed up, it never failed that he would swoop her out of her bad mood by simply being there.

She wanted to get comfortable with flirting again. She'd blown it bad last night. *Really* bad, if she was going to have to apologize to Delaney. Brody had already helped her feel more desirable with a few simple words. Maybe he could help with some of the rest.

She bit her bottom lip.

"I know that gnawing the lip thing," he said. "What the hell are you thinking?"

Should she even dare? She eyed him. It was a huge favor to ask. "I think I could use a little coaching."

"On what?"

"Dating, of course."

If his head had jerked back any farther, it would've fallen off. "You don't need—"

"Think about it," she interrupted. Now that she'd put it out there, she was really warming to the idea. What better way to ease back into singlehood after eight long years than with someone she had always been comfortable around. "Last night, I drank so much because I was trying to loosen myself up. I kept getting tongue-tied when a guy would come up to me. I won't have to drink if I practice a little. Do you know I haven't danced with a guy since…damn. My wedding."

"Are you serious?"

"Dead serious. You're safe. Didn't you say I needed to be safe? What better person to help me get out of the rusty and into the polished than a guy that sees me as his best friend's ex-wife." She smiled. This really could work.

"Right. That's exactly how I see you, and I'm not the person to do this, Scarlett."

"Because of Ryan."

A lengthy pause followed before he said, "Yeah, because of Ryan."

Deflated, she sighed. Oh well. It was worth a shot.

"It was a stupid idea. I'll just do it the way all women do—trial by fire. Just without the booze." She scooted off the bed and stood up, wincing slightly as her stomach protested the movement. "I need to get back to my room and talk to Delaney. Where're my clothes and I'll get out of your hair."

He stepped outside for a second then returned with her dress.

After going into the bathroom to change, she returned to the other room and found Brody standing ramrod straight, staring outside. He muttered something under his breath and shoved his large hands through his thick, dark hair.

"You okay?" she asked.

He jerked and turned his head in her direction. "Uh, yeah. Fine. Just thinking."

By the looks of it, it was something big. "You just listened to me. Need to talk?"

Again his gaze strayed outside and away from her. "Nah. Just work shit. No big deal."

"All right. Thanks again. I owe you one." As she closed the door, she had the crazy notion that Brody was lying to her. Something about the way he'd avoided her gaze just didn't ring true with his excuse.

But what kind of issue could he have with her?

• • •

Brody slung a beach towel over his shoulder as he made his way across the sand toward the huge resort pool about a hundred yards away. The beat of steel drums mingled with people's laughter and conversations. All he wanted to do was find a nice shady spot under one of the oversize canary-yellow umbrellas, put in his earbuds, and forget about this morning.

He'd been way too tempted to take Scarlett up on her offer.

Way. Too. Tempted.

He wasn't in the right frame of mind to do what she'd asked. Not only because of his unresolved feelings for Scarlett, but because he was fucking furious with Ryan for lying to him, not to mention how it sounded like he'd used Brody to cover up his cheating. Fucking asshole. That wasn't cool, on so many levels, and made him see red every time he thought about.

A feminine voice shrieked from behind him. "Oh, thank God, there you are!"

Closing his eyes, Brody stopped and hung his head back, letting a defeated sigh breeze past his lips. He'd done well to avoid Tessa all day. It was time to pay the piper.

"What's up, little sis?" he asked with his back still to her.

She rounded him with the same manic look she'd had yesterday. Her blond hair was frazzled, signaling she'd been fisting her hands in it. Everything light where he was dark, she was the complete opposite of him looks-wise. Hell, personality-wise as well. He took a much more laid back approach to life. Tessa had to plan every damn second or she felt like she wasn't in control. Heaven for-freaking-bid she had one second she wasn't in control. The world would end.

"Did you go for your last fitting this morning?" she demanded without preamble.

"Oh." He grimaced, shoving his sunglasses to rest on the top of his head. "Damn. Nope. Totally forgot about it. I'll do it later."

"Brody!" She lightly popped him on the arm. "The wedding is in two days. We need to make sure that the tux place sent the correct suits. If one tux doesn't fit, then everything is ruined." Tears welled in her eyes.

He was a schmuck. He'd only meant to tease her, not make her cry.

"Calm down," he said, giving her a quick brotherly squeeze. "I went. The tux fit. The world is not ending." He studied her for a moment. Dark circles stained the skin under eyes. When was the last time she'd slept? "What's going on? This is overly-obsessive even for you. Just chill out. Nick has everything covered so you can relax. How about just doing that?"

"Relax?" She stared at him as if he'd just suggested they take a trip to the moon. "How am I supposed to relax, knowing the amount of money Nick has shelled out for this wedding?"

"Jesus, Tessa. If something goes wrong, it's his money he's losing. It's not your bank account. Stop worrying."

Her shoulders slumped. "Worrying and second-guessing are all I've done for days."

That sounded nothing like his normally self-assured sister, who never made a decision without being completely certain it was the best one for her. "Tessa, what's going on?"

Tears rimmed her eyes, but she glanced away and crossed her arms. "Nothing."

Yeah, fucking right. Big brother roared to the surface, and he puffed out his chest. "Do I need to kick someone's ass?"

Namely a fiancé.

"Take it down a peg, Brody. I'm not fifteen anymore. If anyone needs their ass kicked it's me, for jumping into this without knowing all the facts."

"What facts?"

She was silent for a long moment before she looked up at him, her blue eyes moist. "Nick doesn't want kids."

All Brody could do was blink at her, unable to comprehend what she was saying. "Doesn't want kids? Goddamn, Tessa. That's a huge thing not to talk about. How did you get this far without discussing it?"

"I thought we had. We discussed having kids in the future. Nick was always clear he wanted to wait a few years so we could have time just the two of us first. I agreed, because I do love the idea of us traveling with no real responsibility before we settled down and became parents. But in hindsight, I think that was his way of telling me."

"Waiting a few years and not wanting kids are two totally different things. We come from a fucking huge family. He knows that. How could he think you'd ever be okay with not having children?"

He wanted a whole goddamn house full of kids. He had five sisters, one older and four younger, all stair-stepped in age. And he couldn't image not giving his future kids the same kind of loving, large family he'd been raised in. Tessa had always felt the same.

"He hoped that by time we got a few years out, I'd have changed my mind."

His mouth popped open, and he shook his head. Starting a marriage off based on a lie was building their life together on a shaky foundation. At least the ass had told her before they exchanged vows. "If he kept it secret this long, what finally made him admit the truth?"

"He got drunk the night before we flew out here. A friend of mine posted on Facebook that she was pregnant, and when I saw it, I mentioned it to Nick. His response was a grimace and a 'there goes her life.' That opened up the conversation."

"Wow, Tessa. What're you going to do?"

"What can I do? Do you have any idea how much he's paid for this wedding?"

"Fuck that. If you don't want to marry this guy, don't. It's that simple."

"But it's not. I love him, Brody. I really do. Deeply. I don't know if I can give up kids to be with him, though. You know how badly I want to be a mom one day. You feel the same about being a dad."

He did, and the idea of never being one was unfathomable.

"You have two days to figure this out before you walk down the aisle. I highly recommend that you use this time to do some deep soul-searching instead of worrying over every little detail of this wedding." He stooped to look her directly in the eyes. "This is a huge decision. If you take your vows, you're accepting a childless marriage. Can you do that?"

"I don't know," she said, barely above a whisper. "What if I can't?"

"Then you come to me, and I'll get you out of here."

"I love him, Brody."

"I have no doubt you do, but this issue won't just go away once you get married. You can't bank on hope that he'll one day change his mind. You have to accept, and if you can't, you need to walk away."

A sad smile turned up one corner of her mouth. "How is such a confirmed bachelor so schooled on love and relationships?"

"I may be single, but I have always believed in marriage. Blame Mom and Dad."

"Blame us for what?" a deep voice asked from a distance, marking the abrupt end of their conversation.

Brody glanced over his shoulder to see his tall, white-haired father beside his short, brunette wife, walking toward them hand-and-hand. It had always been that way. The two of them facing everything together. Which wasn't saying that they hadn't had their ups and downs. They had. When he'd been a pre-teen, there had been a time when he'd worried his parents would divorce.

His mother had dealt with some serious depression and anger after giving birth to his stillborn brother—his only brother. His parents had fought a lot back then. But each bump only seemed to make them more solid as a couple when the road leveled back out. It had always shown Brody that marriage wasn't about just loving someone. It was about growing with someone through all the shit life had to throw at you.

"I'm just blaming you for setting a high standard for marriage."

His dad draped his arm around his wife and squeezed her close to his side. "Marriage is work, but if you've married the right one, you're never putting in the work alone."

His mom smiled up at her husband then glanced at her children. "We're getting ready to hit the casino. Anyone want to join us?"

"I'm heading to the pool." He glanced at his sister. "Tessa?"

She hesitated for a moment, then she nodded slightly to herself. "I think I'm going to see about getting a massage."

Brody squeezed his sister's arm in support, and she sent him a soft smile.

"You kids have fun. We'll catch you later." His parents walked past them, still holding hands. Brody couldn't help but smile.

"Go get your massage. Remember, if you need anything, come to me."

"Thanks, big brother."

"Always have been, always will be." He placed a kiss on the top of her head then continued on to the pool.

After he picked a lounge chair and spread his beach towel over it, he sat down, lowered his sunglasses onto his nose, popped in his earbuds so the steel drums were drowned out by the Avett Brothers, then leaned back with a relieved sigh.

Tessa would hopefully chill out some now, which only left one woman to drive him bat-shit crazy while he was here.

A flash of blond caught his peripheral vision. He muttered a string of curses. Could he not get one second of peace?

Scarlett and Delaney were spreading their beach towels on a pair of lounge chairs across the pool directly in front of him. Brody crossed his arms and resisted the urge to go over.

That didn't stop him from soaking in the vision Scarlett made in the colorful sarong she wore tied with a knot between her breasts. The hem barely covered the tops of her thighs and gave him an enticing glimpse of her beautiful legs. She kept toying with the knot that kept the sarong closed, that plump bottom lip caught between her teeth. Finally she sat down without taking the cover off. Delaney shook her head and motioned for her to stand. He guessed by the ease between the two that they had made up.

When Scarlett remained where she was, a frustrated Delaney snapped her fingers then clapped her hands. Scarlett blew out a breath and shoved to her feet. Again, her hands hesitated on the knot.

What the hell was she wearing underneath that cover?

Anticipation scurried through him, and he cursed it to hell and back. Thinking about this woman in that way had always and would always be wrong. But for the life of him, he could not drag his eyes away from her as she fought for the courage to take off that blasted cover.

Finally, she gave the knot one sharp tug and the fabric fell away.

Holy. *Fuck*. Everything in him stilled as she revealed a black, barely-there string bikini.

Yeah, he'd caught a glimpse of her in her bra and panties last night, but he hadn't allowed himself a full-on perverted look while she'd been lying there unconscious. Now his eyes couldn't get enough. The damn material barely covered anything. All he saw was skin, skin, and more skin. And he wasn't the only dude noticing her, either.

How could this woman doubt for one second she was hot? How could she have hesitated in taking that wrap off? She should be owning that with an air that said flat out, *Look, but don't touch.*

There was something extremely wrong about the fact that she didn't, that she was awkward in her skin and in her own beauty, and it didn't set well with him at all. He'd never thought of Scarlett as insecure. But the woman he'd known had always been with Ryan—and she sure didn't dress like this. At least she was trying to embrace her beauty by venturing outside her typical attire, but she was nowhere near to owning the new look.

A man came over to them. A tight smile came to Scarlett's lips while Delaney easily started a conversation with him. Everything about Scarlett was tense and unwelcoming. It was no wonder she'd resorted to having a couple of drinks last night to loosen up.

As much as he liked the idea that her awkwardness would keep men at bay, he hated seeing her so outside her element. She should have men lining up to be with her.

Body language said a lot, and the man gave up and walked away. Scarlett instantly brought her knees to her chest, covered her face with her hands, and shook her head. Delaney patted her on the shoulder and said something, most likely a bold-face lie that the encounter hadn't been as bad as Scarlett thought.

Brody sucked his teeth. That had gone horribly, and she knew it. She'd said all she wanted to do was practice flirting, but what if she reached for the alcohol again? Last night had come close to disaster. Hell, he'd seen the horror on her face when she worried they'd slept together.

It was evident she had no intention of fucking anyone while she was here. Why was that?

She'd talked a lot of smack in his room about being over her marriage and over Ryan, but she'd just found out about his affair, and her emotions were raw. She was rightfully hurt. However, some marriages were able to work past infidelity. If there was one couple he thought could do it, it was Ryan and Scarlett.

If she ended up getting shit-faced and doing something stupid like she almost had last night, that would just add more hurt and guilt to their problems.

She asked for a safe man.

To her, he was safe.

Still, he made himself stay where he was and watch. A few other men approached the girls. Delaney was welcoming, but Scarlett never wavered from her aloof attitude. Each man ended up focusing on Delaney while Scarlett looked around, the obvious third wheel.

After the last guy kissed the top of Delaney's hand and gave Scarlett an awkward nod, Brody had seen more than he needed to. He stood up and walked over to them.

Scarlett lowered her sunglasses down her nose. "Brody. Hey."

He stood at the end of her lounge chair and hesitated for just a brief moment. It wouldn't be the first time he'd spent time alone with her. He'd done it plenty of times in the past without anything ever happening, not even a lingering weird glance. This would be no different. "Tonight. Seven o'clock."

The grin she gave him should have made him feel good. All it did was make him certain he would regret ever agreeing to this.

Chapter Four

Why was she so nervous?

Scarlett fidgeted with the hem of her skirt. It was just Brody. They had been out plenty of times in the past, just the two of them. Brody had embraced her presence the moment Ryan had introduced her as his girlfriend. Over the years, they'd formed their own friendship outside of Ryan. It had been nice. They'd meet for lunch or catch a matinee when Ryan wasn't available to take her.

Yeah, he was Ryan's best friend, and she really had no idea how Brody felt toward her ex, whether he felt betrayed in his own way that Ryan had never confided in him. But one thing was clear—he did not condone his friend's action. There was some comfort in that. It made her feel less alone than she had before. Delaney, of course, would have her back. But she hadn't been counting on Brody's support. It went to show what kind of man he really was.

She glanced at the clock.

Ten to seven. She took a deep breath.

"Chill out, chick. You're acting like you're going on a real date."

"I know. It's stupid, right?"

Delaney eyed her. "Nah. I like that Brody is going to get you out there and feeling comfortable again—without the excess booze."

Earlier, Scarlett had groveled for forgiveness from her friend. Delaney had brushed the matter aside as if it wasn't a big deal, stating it wasn't like Scarlett hadn't had a few run-ins with the devil-horned Delaney in the past, mostly when Scarlett had been encouraging her to leave her ex. So last night's incident was swept under the rug with the promise that they'd have a killer rest of the trip.

"I feel bad about leaving you up here by yourself."

Delaney waved her hand and made a *pftt* sound. "About what? The room service I'm about to gorge myself on, or the in-house massage I ordered? I'm looking forward to a night in. As much as I love being in the beautiful Bahamas, it doesn't mean I want to do something every night. There's only so much clubbing and drinking a girl can do. We'll do something tomorrow night. Besides, we have to get up early in the morning to go snorkeling."

Scarlett was really looking forward to that. She had never been snorkeling. The adventure they'd picked was an additional charge, but had come highly recommended by everyone.

"As long as you don't care."

"Seriously, go get your groove back. Besides there are worse things in the world than having to look across the table at Brody Minton."

"Do you have the hots for him?" Scarlett asked, surprisingly unsettled by the idea.

"I won't lie, I wouldn't mind spending a night on that man's arm. There's something more to him than your typical guy."

"I could probably hook you up on a date." Why did she not like that?

The only real explanation was that Brody had always been hers, in a way. She'd missed him over the last year, had even tried getting him to go places with her. But after the sixth "rain check," she'd stopped asking.

Delaney shrugged. "We still have a few days here. We'll see how things go."

A tap came from the door, and Scarlett's heart picked up speed. She had to chill out, like Delaney said. These kinds of nerves were only asking for a night as dreadful as the last.

She opened the door and was shocked at the flutter that hit her stomach. Brody was dressed in a pair of dark denim designer jeans and a fitted polo shirt that hugged his strong shoulders and stretched across his wide chest. His longish dark hair was styled back from his forehead.

His light brown eyes lowered over her. She couldn't tell by his expression if he approved of what he saw. Unlike the dress from last night, where the fabric had clung and dipped, she'd decided on a flirtier outfit for this occasion. The strapless floral dress hit mid-thigh, a look she'd finished off with strappy heels.

It was much more a cutesy dress than it was seductive. More her speed. She'd jumped too quickly into the seductive pool twice now and didn't have the confidence to back it up yet. Today by the pool had been a disaster, especially if Brody had given in and agreed to be her mentor. He had to have seen how horrible she was around men.

"*Damn* girl," he said in a very appreciative voice.

A grin spread across her lips. Okay. She could get used to this.

"Shall we?" he asked, offering his arm.

She sent Delaney a smile before stepping out in the hall and closing the door behind her. She took his arm. "Let's."

They walked down the hall in silence for a few moments. Finally she asked, "What do you want to do tonight?"

"I've got it all planned out. You just relax and enjoy."

She could get used to this, too. Ryan had never been much of a date planner. From the time they'd started dating, his go-to had always been, "whatever you want, babe." So she ended up always making the plans for them. This was a very nice change.

They stepped outside and followed a stone path toward the beach. It didn't take much to realize where they were going to eat dinner. The resort offered a quaint seaside restaurant. It wasn't one of the more upscale dining places, but when she'd passed it the first time, she thought it would be a great spot to have dinner and watch the sun set.

When they reached the open air restaurant, Brody led her to one of the picnic tables. A white cloth covered the wood. The small space was set up for dinner and had a more elegant atmosphere than the "beach bum" feel it had for lunch. Tiki torches had been lit and the shades lowered around them, except for the section facing the water, where the orange glow of the sun brightened the horizon.

"I know this isn't the nicest restaurant here. But I thought we could have dinner and watch the sun set."

She blinked at him, stunned that he'd had the exact same thought she'd had. Not that the idea was unique. Plenty of people probably had the same notion when they saw this restaurant for the first time. But to be so in sync with the person she was dining with was so outside her usual experience, and it was oddly exciting.

After they sat down, she picked up the menu. So far the food at the resort had been amazing, and she was determined to try something different at each meal. At home, she was rarely this adventurous. She always stuck with old favorites she knew she'd enjoy. Here, she could try anything under the sun, and if she hated it, that was okay—she'd just pick something else.

Once the waiter had taken their orders—her blackened snapper with lemon caper sauce, and Brody's New York strip with blue cheese butter—she linked her fingers and laid them on top of the table, leaning forward. "So what have you been up to the last year?"

Brody took a sip of his beer before saying, "Not much, really. Training my ass off."

"I watched your fight a few months ago."

A pleased smile turned up his lips. "You did? With Ryan?"

The mention of her ex caused her stomach to twist. Clearing her throat, she lightly shook her head. "I may be a novice to this dating thing, but I've read an article that advised against talking about your ex on a first date. So let's not mention the R word the rest of night, okay?"

"You're right," he said with a sharp nod. "Force of habit. I apologize."

"No need. Just putting it out there. But to answer your question, no, I didn't watch it with him. He was on a business trip." Now she knew what those "business trips" meant, and there was no way Brody didn't, either.

But there was no pity in Brody's warm eyes; if anything he seemed more pleased than he had a few moments ago. "So you watched it on your own, huh?"

"Why do you sound so surprised?"

"In all the years I've known you, Scarlett, I can count on one hand the times you've watched a fight."

True. It wasn't that she had anything against Mixed Martial Arts. She didn't. It was definitely a respectable sport, but she just couldn't get into it like she could football. Now, *that* was her sport.

"There was nothing else on television."

Brody laughed, and she grinned in response. Gosh, she

hadn't realized how much she'd enjoyed that sound until this very moment.

"That's more like it."

"I'd heard you were dating a veterinarian a while back."

"I thought we weren't talking about exes?"

"*My* ex...unless your story comes with some serious baggage."

"Nah." Brody waved off the comment. "It was never like that. I wasn't dating Julie as much as I was letting her use me to make her now-fiancé jealous."

"What kind of woman—" She stopped mid-sentence when he held up his hand.

"She had no idea I was letting her use me. *She* had no idea she was using me. She was trying for an actual relationship. But I knew the minute I showed up on our first date and her best friend opened the door—there were some unresolved feelings there. So I decided to have a little fun."

"What did you do?"

"Just made Tommy realize that he had a good woman beside him, and if he didn't snatch her up, someone else would."

"So you played matchmaker?"

He shrugged. "A little."

"So, you're a romantic."

"Maybe a smidge," he said, with another shrug and a half-grin.

The waiter returned with their food and placed their plates in front of them. The blackened fish smelled fantastic, but the hunk of medium-rare beef on Brody's plate looked absolutely amazing. She should've ordered the steak, damn it. She cut into her fish with her fork and took a bite. Lemon with a spicy kick flooded her taste buds. It was definitely delicious, something she'd be glad she tried, but old favorites were old favorites for a reason—it was the steak that was making her mouth water.

Brody shoved a forkful of the meat into his mouth, closed his eyes and groaned. "Shit. This place knows how to cook a cow."

Rub it in why don't you. As she was raising her fork for another bite, Brody cut a nice-sized portion of his steak and put it on her plate. She froze. "What're you doing?"

"I've watched you eye my meal since the waiter placed it in front of me. I'm sharing."

Her mouth popped open in surprise. "You're sharing?"

"Yep."

She glanced down at her fish, then used her fork to cut a chunk off. Brody immediately shook his head. "No, thank you. I'm not a fan of snapper."

"But you just gave me big part of your meal."

"It's okay, really. I want you to enjoy your meal."

All she could do was stare at him. The gesture was just so sweet. Not that she'd never had someone do sweet things for her—Ryan had, especially the first few years of her marriage—but it'd been a long time since a man had worried about her needs first. Brody looked up from his plate.

A jolt hit her low in the stomach as his caramel-colored eyes met her gaze. Well, that was different. But it wasn't scary. Honestly, it felt right. It made sense. She'd always felt a special connection with Brody—it would be only natural for attraction to seep in now that she was single.

The longer they stared at each other, the more the air between them thickened. "Thank you," she finally said.

Brody swallowed and glanced away. So, he'd felt it, too. She couldn't tell how *he* felt about it, though.

He popped another piece of steak into his mouth and chewed. "I thought we'd go dancing after dinner. What do you think?"

She didn't like the way he was avoiding her gaze now.

Yeah, that had been a weird moment. "That sounds like fun."

"Maybe you can dance with a few different men tonight."

He still hadn't looked at her, and she slowly lowered her fork back onto her plate. "I thought you were going to give me some coaching tonight."

His gaze darted up to her then skated away again. "I am, but I can't see how dancing with me is going to be any help at all. Dinner has proved you're too comfortable with me. Dating, especially first dates, are rarely, if ever, comfortable, especially at the start of the date. You need to practice with strangers."

There wasn't anything comfortable about what had sparked to life between them a moment ago. That had been excitingly *un*comfortable. Why was he pushing her off on another man? "But—"

"I'll be there. You'll still be safe. If you start to feel overwhelmed we can come up with a signal, and all you have to do is give it, and I'll step in. Sound good?"

She blew out a breath. Maybe she'd been wrong. Maybe he hadn't felt it. God knew, she was horrible at picking up on cues. Or…maybe he had, and it freaked him out so much that he was making sure to put distance between them. Either way, it was clear he wanted her to focus on other men and not him. Disappointment settled on her chest, which was crazy. "Yeah. Sounds good."

"It's a plan then," he said. "They're having a dance party tonight around the pool. I'll stand watch, and you go mingle your hot ass off." He popped the meat in his mouth and gave her a pressed-lip smile before he chewed.

"What about you?" she asked as she took a bite of the steak Brody had put on her plate. Though it tasted heavenly, it lay heavy on her tongue, and she had a hard time swallowing it.

"What about me?"

"Are you going to mingle your hot ass off?"

"I think I might."

And if that didn't just make everything perfectly clear. Brody had no interest in her as a woman. Not that it should surprise her. Hadn't it been the way for years now with her own husband?

There had to be someone on this damn island that found her attractive, and not because she was two sheets to the wind. She planned to put everything she had in dancing tonight.

• • •

If he had to watch her dance with one more fucker, he was going to punch something. Brody raked a hand over his face, trying to rein in the jealous green monster that was pretty much screaming at him to go rip her away from the fourth man who'd asked her dance.

At dinner, his advice that Scarlett dance with others had seemed like a wise idea. Especially because, after all these years, it'd finally happened—the lingering, heated glance. He'd felt it all the way to his fucking balls, and he'd blurted out the dancing idea.

It'd been one of dumbest suggestions to come out of his mouth.

But the sexually charged moment had been mutual. It was one thing for him to deal with a one-sided attraction to Scarlett. But having her share in it made everything a whole lot harder. Add in the fact that she looked so goddamn beautiful with the ocean behind her and her blond hair blowing gently in the wind, and for the first time ever, he worried he wouldn't be able to keep his hands off her. Worried he was going to do something he couldn't take back. And it scared the shit out of him.

Because he would *not* be the man she used to get even

with her husband. She had just found out Ryan had been cheating on her. She wasn't in her right mind.

But he was.

And he refused to be a regret of hers because of something she'd done in the height of fury. If that meant he had to use every goddamn bit of inner strength to make her believe he only saw her as his best friend's wife, then by God, he would. Even if it killed him to push her to flirt with other men.

He scrubbed his face with his hand.

Why did it have to be Scarlett? Why couldn't he feel this way about any other woman on the planet besides that woman?

It wasn't like he hadn't tried. He'd dated. Did the same damn thing Julie had done to try and get over Tommy. But Julie's situation had turned out differently. She was in love with her best friend, and Tommy had eventually opened his stupid eyes and had fallen in love with her.

Maybe he needed to try a little damn harder. Maybe he needed to have his own fling to keep himself occupied while he was trapped on this godforsaken island with Scarlett.

Yeah, that definitely sounded good.

He scanned the area. Tiki torches outlined the perimeter of the pool, and everything was cast in a slightly orange glow. A lot of the people here were already coupled off, having come on a weekend getaway with their husbands or boyfriends. But there was still a pretty good selection of single ladies, all bronzed from the sun and gorgeous. Not a damn one interested him.

His gaze strayed to Scarlett, who was sober as sober could be but having a grand ol' time with Mr. Doofus. Brody had coined that name when the guy had come up to her. He was definitely not one of the pretty boys who walked around like a puffed up peacock. The guy seemed more of the stereotypical accountant type—wire-rimmed glasses, super polite, gentlemanly…or, as Scarlett would put it—safe.

It grated on Brody's fucking nerves.

God, this had been a horrible idea. He just wanted to get this night over with, go back to the room, and have a beer—alone. His cell phone vibrated in his pocket, and he pulled it out, glancing at the name.

Ryan.

The bastard had been calling Brody back since last night. He hadn't answered. He still wasn't sure what he was going to say to him, and he was too angry right now to have any sort of conversation with the dickhead. He had no proof that Ryan had used him to cover his cheating, but he was beyond furious at being lied to. *Happy marriage, my ass.*

He would eventually have to confront his friend. Maybe give him a serious smack on the back of the head for being a fucking moron. Maybe that would knock some sense into the idiot.

His phone dinged indicating a text message, and Brody rolled his eyes.

He swiped his thumb across the lock screen then pressed the message icon.

Stop dodging my calls.

Working his neck from side to side, Brody clicked the phone off, shoved it back in his pocket and refocused on Scarlett, who was now slow dancing to an old eighties ballad with Mr. Doofus. She had her arms looped around his neck, and he had his palms resting respectably on her hips. She was looking up at him, and they were talking. Seemed to be an easy conversation.

Fucking great.

It was one thing to watch her with her husband. But a new man was excruciating. Was this how Tommy had felt while Brody dated Julie? He'd known Tommy would get jealous, which was why he played up more attraction to Julie than he'd really felt. But a part of him now felt bad for the guy.

Because this sucked. It gnawed. Ached. Made him want to snatch her away. No wonder Tommy had eventually decked him good.

He sure as fuck could knock the shit out of this guy, and he wasn't doing a damn thing.

Dude. Distract yourself.

"You're Brody 'The Iron' Minton, aren't you?" said a soft, feminine voice.

He glanced over to find a petite, pretty brunette in a slinky black dress, eyeing him. He smiled. Yeah, he could work this.

"At your service."

She smiled. "I thought so. You have on long sleeves so I couldn't see your rad tat for confirmation."

Wherever he went, his sleeve was a topic of conversation. He was damn proud of the piece. The artist had taken his love for comic books and inked a realistic layout of his favorite Marvel superheroes over his entire arm. "Since you know about my tattoo, I'm taking it you're a fan."

"Hell yeah, I'm a fan."

She was a little younger than he preferred. Probably early twenties. Probably still in college. But definitely perfect distraction material.

"Who're you here with?"

"Girl's trip." She waved at a group of five ladies standing in the corner, who giggled as soon as he glanced over. "We're living it up some before we all go our separate ways again in a few weeks."

"College?" he asked.

"Yes! How did you know?"

"Lucky guess."

"Well, I'm the designated spokesperson for the group. The rest of them are too shy for their own good. But we saw you standing here alone, we'd love it if you'd join us, maybe take some pictures with us. Rita has a boyfriend who's a superfan of yours, and he'll be jealous as hell if we come back with evidence we hung out with the great MMA fighter."

Brody chuckled. At least his fans still believed he was great, even if his coach didn't. Besides, he'd wanted a distraction. This sure as hell was going to keep him preoccupied.

"Sure. I'd love to."

"Really?!" She clapped her hands excitedly. "That's so super cool of you!" Then she turned to her friends and yelled, "He said yes!" which got a peel of squeals from the group.

The attention pumped him up. Scarlett had kept him from worrying about his career and what he was going to do when he got home. Now these girls would keep him from overthinking about Scarlett.

"My name is Whitney, by the way."

"It's nice to meet you, Whitney."

He followed her to her friends and was immediately enveloped by five gorgeous women talking over each other. He politely listened to their gushing over his last fight, how much they were fans, and how jealous their boyfriends would be. He posed for pictures with them and then asked a person nearby to get a group shot of all of them.

For the most part he was distracted, but he did his duty to Scarlett and kept an eye on her. Not that she seemed like she needed it. She and Mr. Doofus were now sitting in a booth, chatting away.

He refocused on the girls, allowing them to tell him their life stories until he felt a tug on his shirt. A glance around brought him face-to-face with Scarlett. Immediately, his heart jumped, and, like he had thousands of times before, he cursed the instant reaction.

"Looks like things are going well with you," he said.

"I can say the same thing about you." She eyed the girls.

"I didn't know the cheerleader sorority type was your kind of thing."

The comment caused a ripple of pleasure, and he narrowed his eyes. "Am I detecting a bit of jealousy, Scarlett?"

Shrugging, she glanced off to the side. "Perhaps. They make me feel old."

Old? Yeah, she might have a few years on them, but that was it. Her beauty could never compare to any other woman's—or at least he'd yet to find one who did. "You shouldn't feel old."

She sighed and met his eyes. "I miss being that age. Young. Just go with the flow. No worries."

"Yeah. Me, too."

"I'm sorry. I didn't meant to barge in. I think I'd like to call it a night."

He shifted his body more toward her. "Why? I thought you and Mr.—uh, the guy you've been dancing with—were hitting it off."

"Yeah. I did, too, until his girlfriend texted him and asked where he was."

Brody grimaced. "Damn."

"Why are men such pigs?"

"We're not all pigs."

"A vast majority of you are." He caught a sheen of her eyes as she crossed her arms protectively over her chest.

She was so new to the dating game again.

"Give me a minute, and I'll walk you back to your room."

"No," she waved her hand. "I just wanted to tell you where I was going. You stay and have fun."

"Absolutely not, Scarlett. I wanted you to dance with other men," he forced out. "Just give me a second."

He stepped back to the women and said his good-byes to a chorus of disappointed groans. When he turned back to Scarlett, she had her fingers linked together and was looking anywhere but at him or the women. It wasn't hard to pick up on how uncomfortable she was. Nothing about tonight had gone the way it was supposed to.

And it was his fault.

He was supposed to be showing Scarlett a good time, letting her think she was reacquainting herself with single life in a comfortable, safe way. Instead, one moment of freak-out, and he'd thrown her to the wolves, and because of that, she'd had another bad experience with another piece of shit man.

He stepped up beside. "How about a walk on the beach?"

She glanced up at him, a grateful smile on her face. "That would be nice. Thank you."

And this would be his biggest test yet.

She's off-limits, Minton. Remember that.

• • •

Scarlett stopped at the edge of the soaked sand and let the water lap up over her feet as the waves came in and out. Closing her eyes, she leaned her head back and let the ocean breeze flow over her.

Tonight had sucked.

She couldn't believe it when that guy pulled his phone from his pocket and muttered, "Shit, she woke up." Then he'd looked up at her. "Sorry. I thought my girlfriend had drunk enough to be out cold for the night. Gotta go."

That was it. He hadn't even seemed ashamed of what he'd done, just worried he was going to get caught. Was this what she had to look forward to?

Were men even capable of being faithful?

A slight touch to her wrist caused goose bumps to rise on her arms, and she glanced over at Brody.

"Are you okay?" he asked.

They'd been walking on the beach for ten minutes. Her

strappy sandals dangled from his hand. Such a gentleman. At least he was one of the good ones. So there was hope that all men weren't jerks.

"Yeah. I'm fine. Just a little defeated."

"You can't let one incident get you down."

"I know, but after everything"—she shrugged—"I just needed something to go right." She scrunched her nose at him. "Does that make sense?"

He nodded. "It does, but looking for anything more than a fling here really isn't practical."

She turned toward him. "I'm not looking for a fling, and I'm definitely not looking for a relationship. I just wanted to remember what it was like to flirt."

"Well, didn't you? It seemed like you and that guy were having a good time."

"We were. I was comfortable around him. He made me laugh. He was attractive."

Brody's jaw tightened, and he turned his attention to the large expanse of black water before them. "Then, you got exactly what you were looking for, Scarlett."

If she looked at it that way, she guessed she did. When it came to being single, she wasn't sure what she wanted. She sure as hell wasn't ready to jump into a new relationship, but she couldn't lie and say that finding out that guy had a girlfriend hadn't thrown her completely.

This showed how messed up she was. She couldn't just appreciate what had happened tonight without focusing on the end result. Yeah, the ass had a girlfriend. But she'd smiled, flirted, and danced, all without a drop of alcohol in her system. She'd proven that she could do it. That was what she needed to take from tonight.

She moved closer to Brody, lifted up on her tiptoes, and kissed his cheek. The stubble on his jaw was rough against her lips, but it didn't stop another excited quiver from hitting down low. She inhaled his cologne—a spicy, earthy blend. He'd always worn this cologne. When someone passed by her and she caught a whiff of it, she always thought of him. Because it was just Brody.

She pulled back. "Thank you."

His throat worked, and he shifted away from her. The move hurt, but she brushed it aside. Brody had made it clear over dinner that even if he felt the spark between them, he was not going to act on it. She had to respect that.

Besides, she could use a friend of the opposite sex to help her through all this.

"Are you ready to call it a night?" he asked.

A sad smile came to her lips. No. She could stay out here all night. But it was time to let him off the hook.

"Yeah."

They walked back to her room in silence. As they reached her door, Brody handed her the shoes, and she took them, biting her bottom lip. She wanted to give him a tight hug for everything he'd done for her tonight.

Should she? She didn't want to freak him out more. It was just a hug, though.

All right, she was doing it. She wrapped her arms around his waist and hugged him from the side. He held himself rigid beneath her, then his body relaxed. The heavy weight of his muscular arm settled across her shoulders, and he squeezed her closer.

Before she made him uncomfortable, she pulled back slightly, but his arm prevented her from putting distance between their bodies. As she glanced up, their eyes connected. Heat resided in his gaze, and she froze, her breath catching in her lungs. She couldn't look away.

His arms slipped to her waist, his hand cupping the curve of her hip as his grip tightened. Her heart beat faster. Chest tight, she laid her palm above his pec, and a muscle jumped beneath her hand.

Brody skimmed his knuckles softly across her cheek. "You have no idea," he murmured.

When he didn't elaborate, just grazed her skin again with his knuckles, she whispered, "No idea about what, Brody?"

Blinking, he instantly let his arm fall away from her and then stepped back, rubbing the nape of his neck. What was he talking about? She stepped toward him, but when he took a quick shift away, she froze.

"Brody?"

He shook his head. "Go to bed, Scarlett."

"But—"

"Go to bed." He spun and stalked down the hall.

Watching him go, she replayed what had happened between them in her mind. She may be rusty at reading men, but there was no way she had misinterpreted that moment.

Brody had wanted to kiss her.

And she was shocked by how much she wished he had.

Chapter Five

You have no idea.

Brody raked his hand down his face, then grabbed the tiny glass and shot the whiskey down his throat, enjoying the burn as it traveled to his stomach.

Why had he fucking said that?

With her gazing up at him, all he could think about was that she had no idea how much power she had over him, and the words had spilled out. He'd come so damn close to kissing her the way he'd always wanted. She would've accepted the kiss, too. Then what?

Then they got back to Atlanta, she and Ryan had a long heart-to-heart, and decided they wanted to try and make things work. Yeah, not a road he was interested in traveling.

"Where the hell have you been all day?"

Hiding.

He glanced over as Blake pulled back one of the bar stools and perched on the edge of it. Brody had stayed in his room all day, not wanting to chance bumping into Scarlett. But between Ryan still blowing up his phone, and his thoughts about Scarlett, he'd about driven himself mad. All he wanted was a few drinks to dull his senses.

"Taking it easy today," Brody replied. "Tomorrow's going to be nuts."

Tessa's wedding.

Since they'd gone their separate ways yesterday, he hadn't heard from his sister. He wasn't sure what that meant. Until she came to him, he'd give her space, though. The last thing she needed was big brother breathing down her neck while she made this difficult decision. If she went through with the wedding, he'd support her. If she didn't, he'd be there, too.

"Thank God all I have to do is show up tomorrow." Blake motioned to the bartender then to Brody's shot glass. The guy stepped over, pulled out another glass, and filled both. His cousin turned his head toward him. "So, what's up?"

"What do you mean?"

"Cuz, I've known you since birth. You don't belly up to a bar unless something's bugging you."

Brody sighed. "I've just got a lot on my mind."

"Wouldn't have something to do with a certain blonde hottie, would it?"

"That obvious, huh?" he scoffed softly and shook his head.

"Well, when my usually level-headed cousin suddenly goes guard dog over another man's wife it kind of gets your attention. That goes beyond the best friend duty, bro." Blake shot back his whiskey, and Brody followed suit. "How long have you been feeling her?"

If there was anyone he could trust to talk to, it was Blake. "Too long."

"And where's her husband?"

"Shacked up with someone else."

"That fucker." Blake blew out a harsh breath. "That was what her public meltdown was all about the other night."

"Yeah."

"I wish I could say I was surprised, but Ryan has always been a douchebag."

Blake's feelings for Ryan never made a lick of sense to Brody. The Ryan he knew had always been a genuine friend. "What's your issue with him, man?"

His cousin's jaw tightened. "It was a long time ago."

"No joke. You've had a grudge against Ryan since we were teens. You never told me why."

"It didn't involve you. You and Ryan were solid. He and I had issues. No reason to cause friction between you two because he was a fuckhead."

Curiosity was getting the best of him now. "What happened?"

Blake gestured for another round of shots. "He fucked around with Bianca."

Bianca was Blake's long-term girlfriend in high school. To everyone's shock, including his own, they broke up right before graduation. Blake left town, and Ryan had never mentioned anything to Brody about it. Not that he should be surprised now, not with all the recent lies. "That's why you left town."

"Fuck yeah, that's why I left town. What no one knows is she was pregnant. She let me believe it was mine. Never told me it was possibly Ryan's."

Eyes wide, Brody shifted his body toward his cousin. "She was pregnant?"

"Yep. I was young and terrified out of my mind, but I was excited, too, you know? I loved Bianca. I saw my future with her." He shot the liqueur back and slammed the glass on the table. "She tried to end things with Ryan, which pissed him off. Ryan cheerfully let me know that Bianca had been warming his bed. I confronted her, and she told the truth. She swore that baby was mine. I'll never know if it was. She miscarried a week later."

"Damn, cuz. I'm sorry."

Blake shrugged. "It was a long time ago. It fucked me up for a while, but I joined the Marines and left. Best decision I ever made."

"Do you forgive Bianca?"

"I really don't think about her much at all. Being back in Atlanta this past year I've, of course, heard about her. You can't bump into anyone from the fucking past without them catching you up on every goddamn detail you've missed. She went on to college. Got her degree. Married. Has a kid. I'm happy for her."

"You didn't answer my question."

"What's to forgive? We were young. Stupid. It all worked out the way it was supposed to. I like my life. I can't imagine what it'd be like right now if things had turned out different. Unanswered prayers and all that shit, you know?"

Brody did know. Unfortunately, one of his prayers had been answered and he felt horrible about it.

Two females started singing "Girls Just Want to Have Fun," behind him then broke out into a peel of giggles. Brody stiffened as Blake glanced behind him.

"Well, well, well. Speak of the devil."

Scarlett.

Brody shifted on the bar stool until he faced the small stage. Scarlett and Delaney each had an arm around the other and were singing at the top of their lungs, slurring their words.

"You'd think she wouldn't touch another drink after the other night," Blake muttered.

He was actually thinking the exact same thing.

Scarlett's eyes connected with his. She instantly stopped singing and began waving in an overly dramatic fashion. "Brody! Hey!"

Then she and Delaney laughed again. Brody rubbed his

face, trying to keep from smiling. He didn't like seeing Scarlett drunk again, but there were no men around, and no flirting, so there was no harm in it at this moment.

"She's a beauty," Blake said, crossing his arms across his chest.

"Yes, she is."

"She's free now. I don't see why you can't go after her."

"Except she's Ryan's ex."

Blake's nose scrunched in distaste. "That fucker doesn't deserve your loyalty, dude."

"Ryan has never done anything to me but be a damn good friend. Yeah, I'm starting to see he has a side of him that I don't really care for, but again, he didn't do that to me. Just because he can't keep his dick in his pants, doesn't mean he hasn't been a great friend."

Blake hmphed. "As far as I'm concerned, the moment he put his dick in another woman, his wife became fair game. And you know me—I don't fuck around with married women."

Man, he wished it were that simple. It just wasn't. Blake would never see it the same way Brody did. Not with his feelings toward Ryan. "Yeah, well, I'm not getting between a husband and a wife who have only been separated a few days. That's asking for drama I don't want, especially if they decide to make another go at it after the emotions wear off."

"Now, that's truth."

The girls finished their song and hurried unsteadily toward them. How much had they kicked back already?

Scarlett stopped beside him. "What are you guys up to?"

Blake held up a shot glance and shook it.

"Us, too."

"Uh, Scarlett," Brody hedged. "Is drinking a good idea?"

She laughed and laid her hand on his arm; a thrill shot through him, and he had to force himself not to move away from her touch. "No flirting tonight. Delaney and I had a great day, and it's all about having fun."

Brody ran his fingers through his hair simply to knock off Scarlett's hand. Thankfully it worked, and she didn't seem to notice the move.

"What did you do today?"

"We swam with pigs," Delaney exclaimed, clapping her hands together.

An amused snort came out of Blake. "I've never seen a woman that excited about pigs."

Delaney shot him a look of exaggerated annoyance. "Have you ever swum with pigs?"

"Can't say that I have."

"Then hush it. You have no idea how freaking awesome it is." She fished out her phone, flicked through it, then held up a picture of her and Scarlett laughing as a swarm of pigs swam around them. Technically, they weren't swimming *with* them, just standing in thigh-high water, but who was he to burst her bubble.

A grin spread on Blake's face. "Okay, that does look pretty cool. I might need to check this out before I leave."

"Do so, it's worth the extra cost."

Blake looked over at Brody then back at the girls. "You girls want to join us tonight? See what kind of trouble we can get into?"

Brody glared at his cousin. He sure as fuck didn't need him trying to play hookup. Then he noticed the appreciative way his cousin's gaze roamed over Delaney in her short jean skirt and black halter top. Maybe Blake was trying to get his own hookup. Brody sure as hell wasn't going to cock-block him.

Delaney pursed her lips as her eyes traveled over Blake, returning the heated interest. "Definitely."

Scarlett shot the same look at her friend that Brody had shot at Blake. At least they were on the same page again.

Last night had almost turned disastrous. He couldn't afford a repeat.

"Brody, sing with me," Scarlett said out of nowhere.

He fought a groan. Damn it, he should've expected this. Scarlett loved karaoke. He did, too. Before he'd started keeping his distance, they'd done a lot of duets together... with Ryan watching in the audience. No matter how hard she'd begged, Ryan would never get on that stage. But Brody always had, always mindful of the fact her husband was only a few feet away.

This time wouldn't be the same.

What song would she want to sing? Something lovey-dovey? God, he hoped not.

"Brody?" she said when he remained silent.

"Sure," he finally relented, unable to disappoint her. "What do you want to sing?"

A grin spread her lips, and she did a little happy shimmy, then she took off for the DJ without answering his question. Brody rubbed his face again. Please, let it be a Disney song. "A Whole New World," or "Let It Go." He would gladly get down with some Elsa right now, like he did with his four-year old niece. As long as it wasn't some song that had a secret meaning to him.

A few seconds later, she returned. Her impish expression didn't bode well for him.

"We're next."

She grabbed his hand and tugged him off the stool. He tried to keep his mind off the fact they were holding hands. It wasn't like they hadn't done this plenty of time in the past. Except, now they'd had a moment. A real moment. One full of electricity and heat. And something as innocent as her holding his hand, tugging him along behind her, wasn't so innocent anymore.

When they stepped in front of the microphone stands, she

grabbed hers and he took his.

Then the strummed beat of *Grease*'s "You're The One That I Want" started. He resisted another urge to groan. Just the title said too much about his current frame of mind.

Pushing aside the thought, he brought the mic to his mouth and started singing his lines. And, damn, if he didn't get chills every damn time she touched him. Made him feel like he was losing control with every glance and every goddamn word she uttered.

Scarlett raised the mic then turned and pressed her back into his side as she sang. As much as he wanted her heart to be set on him like the words she sang, he knew that was never going to happen.

God, he was driving himself nuts.

When they reached the chorus, he forced himself to have fun and forget about how each lyric was an echo of his wants. As they *ooh, ooh, oohed*, he swung his hips behind her in the dramatic way John Travolta had in the movie. The amused giggle that interrupted her singing made his chest expand, and he felt a grin come to his lips.

Then she turned, faced him, and slid her hands up her body.

The throaty, seductive purr in her voice telling him to feel her grabbed him right by the balls and refused to let go. He couldn't tear his gaze away from her hands gliding over her breasts. His grip on the mic loosened. He juggled with it before it could hit the floor, missing the next few lines. Once he had it back into a firm grip, he glanced back up at Scarlett, and pure pleasure shined back at him.

He pressed his lips together. She'd done that on purpose. Oh, two could play at this game.

Brody behaved until they got to the last few lines, then he turned toward her, placed his hands low on her hips, and started the Travolta shimmy. He moved toward her as his head lowered toward her chest. She froze for a second, her throat working on a swallow, before she collected herself, wrapped her arms around his shoulders, and shimmied with him. He allowed his hands to rub up and down her hips, enjoying the feel of the silky material of her dress under his hands.

He was playing with fire, and for first time, he didn't give a shit if he was.

Dancing with her, feeling this electricity again, was fucking worth it.

The song came to an end, and the crowd hooted and clapped, but Brody didn't want to let her go. He wanted the song to continue, to stay in this fantasy with her, created by a movie from long ago. But he forced himself to drop his hands and step back.

She stared up at him for a moment then said, "Thank you," and left the stage. He followed, his gaze locked on the sway of her ass. The last couple of shots he'd done with Blake were lowering his inhibitions. He was walking on dangerous ground.

And he wasn't sure if he minded.

• • •

The flying white ball sped straight for Brody's face, and he ducked. Scarlett doubled over as a fit of giggles overtook her.

"You're horrible at this," he said, chuckling.

She had a stich in her side, and she pressed her hand to it. God, she'd missed Brody.

Wanting to listen to one of the live bands, Blake and Delaney had left them alone about two hours ago. Scarlett had no interest in sitting and listening tonight—she wanted to *do*.

Brody had picked up on that, and had offered to go *do* with her so Delaney and Blake could go to the concert. She'd been laughing ever since.

First, they sang a few more songs, then, moved on to darts at another bar. When after ten turns she still hadn't made the stupid dart stick into the board, Brody had taken mercy on her, and they'd moved on to shuffleboard, which they both sucked at. Now, they were trying their hand at table tennis, and Brody kept having to dodge her missiles.

"I never claimed to be good at sports, you know." She grabbed her beer and took a long chug. She'd kept her alcohol consumption under some control and wasn't downing shots like there was no tomorrow. Two drinks an hour. Just enough to lower her usual reserve and let a pleasant buzz warm her insides.

"Okay, one more time," Brody said after he took a swig of his beer.

He set the bottle on a nearby table then tapped the white ball with his paddle so it bounced over to her side. Again, she swiped it harder than she meant to, and it went whizzing toward him. He threw up both arms, protecting his head. The ball bounced off his forearm. "That's it. There's no hope for you."

She snickered and laid her paddle down. "Let's go for a swim."

Ever since they'd come outside, the pool had been beckoning her.

Brody seemed to freeze. "We need bathing suits."

"I have mine on." She waved toward his beige cargo shorts. "And those look like swim trunks to me."

They didn't, but still. It was two in the morning. There was hardly anyone out here. Who was going to say anything?

Yet, he seemed to hesitate.

"Come on, Brody. The pool's packed during the day. We'll have it all to ourselves."

He finally nodded. "It's your night. Let's go."

She did another happy dance, and he laughed. "You are so easy to please."

She stiffened. It'd been a long time since a man had said she was easy to please. Over the last few years, she had been made to believe nothing ever pleased her. That she was always miserable. Nothing was ever good enough.

The thing was, the reason she'd been so miserable was because she'd been alone. Married, but alone. All she'd wanted was Ryan's attention again. To feel a connection with her partner. To not have him come home with flowers, or a necklace, then leave again. She wanted his time.

"Why? Because I want to swim?" she said, trying to brush off the statement.

"Nah. You just want to have fun."

She shrugged and started toward the pool. "Remembering the fun times helps you through the darker ones. All life has them."

He fell into step beside her. "You haven't had a lot of fun lately, have you?"

She evaded the question. "Not in a while."

More like years.

But she didn't want to go there. Not with Brody. He already knew too much about her marriage. He didn't need to know that her infertility had started the demise of their relationship. Since Brody had been unaware of the affair, she had to assume Ryan had never confided in him about that, either.

Typical Ryan, though. Appearances meant a lot to him.

After Ryan said no to more attempts, she'd gone through a very dark, depressing time, trying to accept she was never going to be a mother. While she struggled with her emotions, he took out his frustration at never being a father on her. He grew angry, spiteful…bitter. Became a stranger. She kept looking for glimpses of the man she married, but he was gone.

In hindsight, they should've ended their marriage two years ago. Sometimes it was just hard to call it quits when there was a tiny hope that maybe they'd find common ground again and be able to mend the distance between them.

But then he found himself a fertile woman to replace her with—and they were having a baby.

Ryan was going to be a father. But she wasn't going to be a mother. Bitterness didn't even begin to describe how she felt about that.

"This topic brings me down," she said. "I've had a great night. I'd like for it to end like that."

Without another word, Brody pulled his shirt off over his head. Her throat went dry at the expanse of tanned, toned muscles in front of her. Yep, that was one way to distract her. Her eyes traveled over the comic-book inspired sleeve he sported. She'd always loved that tattoo.

"You've added a new frame, I see."

He held out his arm and ran his finger over the Hulk slamming his mighty green fist into the street. Asphalt sprayed out into the sky, with the caption HULK SMASH! in bright red underneath. He turned his arm over so the underside was showing. Another comic frame contained an amazingly detailed Iron Man with his arms crossed over his chest. Above him in a speech bubble were the words, "We have a Hulk."

She ran the tip of her finger over the ink. "Tony Stark said that, not Iron Man."

"Tony Stark *is* Iron Man," he said with a grin, then he chuckled. "Only you would call me out on that."

She shrugged. "Just saying. When did you get it?"

"About eight months ago. I did it in between fights. I have a couple more frames I'd like to add. One with Hawkeye. Then, of course, Deadpool." He shot her an expectant look.

"Now that I can't wait to see."

Deadpool was her favorite. He knew that, since he used

to take her to all the superhero movies that came out. Ryan abhorred superheroes. But Brody hadn't been there to take her to see *Deadpool*. She'd gone alone…had thought about him, wondered if he was also sitting in a theater somewhere on opening night.

"Hopefully I'll get it finished after this fight."

"When is it?"

"Three months. When I get back, I'll have to throw myself hard-core into training."

"You looking forward to it?"

He grimaced. "This topic brings me down. I've had a great night. I'd like for it to end that way."

His parroted words caused her to chuckle. "Duly noted. Let's swim."

Scarlett unzipped the side zipper on her dress then pushed the shoulder straps over her shoulders. The dress slipped off her frame and pooled at her feet. She then looked at Brody. He stood motionless, his heated gaze locked on her body.

Instantly, her nipples puckered, as desire warmed her blood. Knowing what happened last time things got heated between them, and not wanting this night to end yet, she kicked off her high-heel slides, jogged to the pool, and jumped in, welcoming the cool rush of water that enveloped her.

As she broke the surface, Brody jumped in, causing a huge splash. The water hit her in the face, and she saw the perfect opportunity to make everything playful again. So far tonight, there hadn't been any tension between them, she wanted to keep it that way. She waited until he popped back up. As soon as he did, she used both hands to splash him.

He sputtered then stared at her. "I can't believe you just did that."

Then he retaliated by sending a huge wave her way. Laughing, they both tried to douse each other with as much water as they could. Brody with his large arms and hands won each time. Coming up behind him, she heaved herself out of the water by his broad shoulders and pushed down. He went under easily…too easily.

As he surfaced, he grabbed her around the waist and hauled her to his chest. "That wasn't nice."

Sweeping her up into his arms, he dipped her backward so her head was submerged, then he righted her. As soon as she took a breath, he dunked her again. Water poured down her face and into her mouth, and she sputtered. With one arm tight around his neck, she used the other to clear the water and hair from her eyes.

He went to dunk her under again. Desperate to catch her breath, she folded her other arm around him and kicked loose of his hold. As soon as his arms fell away, she repositioned and wrapped her legs around his waist.

"Uncle," she muttered.

No response came from him. He wasn't moving, either. If anything, he was rigid. She glanced up from the water to his face. Naked heat greeted her. His obvious arousal jutted up, getting acquainted with her butt cheeks. Clinging to him had been a bad move. There was nothing innocent about their position. Brody was between her thighs. Desire flared through her, causing her to throb.

They stared at each other, the air thick. She waited. Would he bolt again? Or would he finally kiss her?

Eyes locked with hers, Brody walked a matter of five steps until her back hit the wall of the pool. His mouth crashed down on hers. Gasping, she tightened her arms around his neck, pulling him closer. His tongue sailed past her lips. Sensations exploded inside her. Never before had she experienced such feelings from a kiss.

Fingers tangled in her hair, then he tugged her head back. The light pain of having her hair pulled sent another jolt of lust slamming through her. His lips skimmed her jaw, down her neck, and over her collarbone. Her breathing escalated, coming in sharp, quick puffs. Every cell of her body was alive, and she wanted to go with it.

He released her hair and moved his hand to her waist, his thumb caressing the skin under the curvature of her breast. She needed him to touch her.

Silently asking, she arched her upper body toward him. He slid his palm up, covering the aching flesh in his large hand. It wasn't enough. She wanted him to devour her. To help her release this tension that was growing wilder with each passing second.

A whimper escaped her lips. He pinched her nipple. In response, she ground against the hard ridge proudly standing between her legs. She'd silently asked once and had gotten what she wanted. Maybe silently asking again…

His entire body stiffened, and his head snapped up from her neck. For a long moment, he stared at her as if he couldn't believe she was actually in his arms. Then he latched onto her legs, tugged himself free, and waded back a good ten feet. He shoved a hand through his wet hair. "Fuck."

Stunned at his one-eighty, she could only blink at him.

He continued to back away. "This can't happen. I'm sorry. That went too far."

"Why not?"

"You know why, Scarlett."

Her damned ex. With everything the son of bitch had done to her, Brody's loyalty to him hurt even more—especially after having a small taste of the way he made her body come alive.

"So, what I want doesn't matter?"

A helpless expression crossed his face. "It's not that simple for me."

Feeling the sting of rejection, she looked away. It was even worse that he was picking Ryan over her. There was an undeniable, intense attraction between Brody and her. She wanted to explore those feelings, embrace the way he made her body feel. After years of having Ryan belittle her in the bedroom, it felt amazing to have her body truly respond to a man again.

And Brody was choosing Ryan.

He must not feel the attraction the same way she did. Not shocking, considering. Brody was a single, extremely hot man. He probably had women climbing in and out of his bed. He hadn't felt dead inside for years. Hadn't just had a reawakening of pure lust.

"I'm sorry, Scarlett."

Tears burned the back of her eyes, but she blinked them away. If he apologized one more time…

She sent him a strained smile. "It's fine. I understand. Don't worry about it."

He hesitated. "I—"

"Just go." She glanced away again, afraid that he would see her pain. That wasn't something she wanted to put on him. He hadn't done anything other than be there for her. This pain was coming from the past, and he didn't deserve the guilt.

Water splashed. She kept her eyes averted until the sound stopped, then she turned to where he'd been. The pool was empty.

And she was alone again.

• • •

The moment Brody slammed the door behind him, he stalked straight to the glass sitting on the mahogany table and swiped it across the room. It crashed against the wall, shattering to the floor

What the fuck had he done?

He shoved a hand through his hair, as he paced. Agitation

made his strides jerky. Though Scarlett had tried to hide her hurt by avoiding his gaze, he'd seen it shining through, crystal clear. He never wanted to be the reason Scarlett felt hurt. Hell, he wanted to give her everything she'd ever desired and more.

He never should've agreed to the fucking swim. The second she'd suggested it, warnings had gone off in his head, screaming that it was a horrible idea.

But *no*.

His stupid ass couldn't disappoint the woman. In the end, he'd done exactly that anyway.

Now he'd crossed the line. At least, *his* line.

He'd finally tasted the forbidden fruit, and like he'd always feared, one sample would never be enough. Her whimpers, her eagerness, had made his dick pulse with need. He wanted more—had used every bit of restraint he possessed to put distance between them, because right there in the pool, in front of any prying eyes, he could've taken her under the veil of water.

He rubbed his lips, her taste still lingered there—the mixture of lager and Scarlett. He could become addicted to that flavor. He feared that one sample had already gotten into his blood.

What the fuck was he going to do?

A light tap came from his door. Every muscle in his body stiffened. Scarlett?

He closed his eyes and tilted his head toward the ceiling. *Don't let it be her.* He didn't have the strength to turn her away again.

Another tap put him in motion. As he wrapped his fingers around the knob, he hesitated for a second before yanking the door open. Air gushed past his lips as he took in his weeping sister.

All thoughts of Scarlett and the mess he'd made were

wiped from his mind as he stepped toward his baby sister, arms outstretched.

"Tessa?" he asked softly.

As a sob rushed out, she pressed her fingers to her lips and hurried into his waiting arms. He immediately enveloped her in a tight hug.

"I want kids," she mumbled against his shirt.

Relief hit him. He would never make decisions for his sisters. Their lives were their own. But Tessa was meant to be a mother. He was thankful she'd chosen her needs over anything else.

He held her for a moment longer then led her into his room. "Big brother's here. I'll take care of everything."

She pressed her face into his chest. "Why can't love be simple?"

That was the question of the day.

"I don't know, sweetie." He kissed the top of her head. "For something that's supposed to be awesome, it sure fucking sucks sometimes."

She titled her head back. "What do you know about love?" There was a teasing tone underneath the sadness in her voice.

He knew more than anyone would ever believe. "Just seen enough with five sisters."

"That you have."

"I have to ask, Tessa. Are you sure?"

"No," she said, honestly. "But I'm certain I can't marry him tomorrow. That's enough for now."

He gestured to the couch—the one where just two nights ago another woman had lain after another man had made her cry. "I'll make the arrangements. You just relax."

Brody pulled out his phone. He hated the pain his sister was in, but she was also giving him an escape. It was a coward's move, but this island was too small for him and Scarlett both.

A few more days and he would really do something stupid that he couldn't, or *she* couldn't, take back.

When an agent answered the phone, Brody said, "I need the first available flight back to Atlanta, Georgia."

• • •

Tessa called off the wedding. Took her home. I hope the rest of your vacation is great.

Scarlett read the missive for the tenth time and flipped the note over to stare at the blank back again.

That was it. How long had he taken to jot that down? Two seconds?

Maybe she should be thankful he'd been thoughtful enough to even write her a note. The convenience of the timing didn't sit well. It seemed to her that Brody had taken the first escape route he'd been given to get the hell off this island.

Coward.

Whatever. Only a few days single, and she was already over the whole man thing. They were too much of a hassle, one she didn't have time or patience for.

As the door to the room creaked open, Scarlett glanced up from Brody's masculine scrawl. Delaney was hunkered down, sneaking into the room with her heels in one hand. Her dark hair was disheveled. Considering it was only five in the morning, she probably expected Scarlett to be fast asleep. As it was, she'd tossed and turned before getting up to watch some TV. Then the sheet of paper had been slipped under the door.

Delaney caught Scarlett watching her. She froze, muttering, "Shit."

"Walk of shame?"

"Shut up." Delaney straightened and closed the door.

"Wow. It *is* the walk of shame. Did you hook up with Blake?"

A pleased, impish expression crossed her friend's face. "I just had the most amazing drunk sex of my life."

Scarlett's mouth popped open. This was a turn of events. "I thought you weren't looking to hook up while we were here."

"I wasn't," Delaney said and shrugged. "It just happened. After we split off, Blake and I had so much fun listening to the band that one thing led to another and we ended up in his room." She bit her lower lip. "That man did things with my body—" She blew out a breath. "*Girl.*"

"No regrets then?"

"Not a damn one. I haven't felt this relaxed in months."

"So, does this mean you're interested?"

"In more than sex? Hell no. I just ended the terrible relationship I was in. If he wants to hook up a couple more times before we leave, I'm totally game, but he's my 'what happens in the Bahama stays in the Bahamas.' I highly recommend getting yourself thoroughly fucked. It does a body good."

Yeah. She'd tried. And failed.

"My night didn't go the same. Brody kissed me and then freaked out."

Delaney's eyes bulged. "He kissed you?"

Scarlett gave her the CliffsNotes version of everything that happened, only getting more detailed when she reached the reason why Brody refused to go any further with her.

"Really? He'd rather stay friends with that douchebag instead of getting a piece of your ass? There's something seriously wrong with him, Scar."

That caused Scarlett to chuckle. God, she loved Delaney. She handed the note to her—she read it quickly then snapped her head up. "He left?"

"Yep."

Delaney crawled up on the mattress and sat cross-legged. "And how do you feel?"

"Honestly? Rejected."

"Yeah, I probably would, too," she said, nodding. "This is on him, babe. Not you." She sat silent for a moment. "I never took Brody for an escape artist, though."

Scarlett sat on the edge of the bed. "I guess I should take it as a compliment that he had to leave an island to keep from doing something he considers stupid."

Delaney laughed. "There ya go! I like that train of thought." She pursed her lips. "What happens when we get home?"

Life would go on. Like usual.

"I went over a year without seeing Brody, and before then it was only because Ryan or I had invited him over. We don't cross paths. He'll be safe in Atlanta."

"I don't think so, honey. Whatever that man is feeling was powerful enough to freak him the hell out. I'd say you've not seen the last of him."

"It doesn't matter. Between Ryan, the dude from the other night, and now Brody, I just want to concentrate on me. I have a lot I need to work on."

"I do, too, girl. Speaking of, are you staying with me once we get back?"

Scarlett blinked. She hadn't even thought about where she was going to live when she got back to Atlanta. After she found out Ryan had been cheating on her, she'd gone straight to her best friend's, crying—more over the baby, which she hadn't shared with Delaney, than the actual end of her marriage—and crashed in the guest bedroom. Four days later, they were using the tickets meant for a surprise romantic getaway with her husband for a seriously needed girl's weekend.

"Are you okay with that?" Scarlett asked.

"Hell yeah, I'm okay with that."

"It'll only be temporary while I find a place of my own."

She waved her hand. "No rush. It'll be fun."

It would be.

What she needed right now was time with her girl, not to complicate her life with men.

With Brody out of the picture, she could now fully concentrate on herself. After she'd found out she was infertile, she'd slipped into a dark funk she couldn't claw her way out of no matter how hard she'd fought against it. That darkness had only grown blacker as Ryan had distanced himself from her. She'd done her best, trying to be what he needed, while ignoring her own needs.

It hadn't worked. He'd still found someone else.

And now she had to find herself.

Chapter Six

Stepping out of the master bathroom, freshly clean and in a pair of fight shorts and logo T-shirt, Brody inwardly groaned at the mouth-watering aroma of brownies teasing his nostrils with their evil, sugary scent.

Tessa was up. Baking. Again.

Man, he was ready for her to go home.

She'd been here for three days. Not only did she test his willpower daily with his ultimate weakness—sweets— she kept reorganizing his shit. His mail had been moved off the end of the marbled granite kitchen counter and into a drawer. She'd rearranged his cabinets, changed where he kept Princess's food bowls and litter box, and shoved the fitness magazines he kept on the coffee table into a wicker basket he didn't even know he'd had and sat them by his couch.

He liked his stuff where he put it.

So far he'd been able to bite his tongue, knowing she was wound tight and needed to keep herself occupied, but if she moved one more damn thing…

Sighing, he rubbed his face. He didn't regret making good

on his promise to her on the island. He'd do anything for his family, and vice versa. Hell, their parents and siblings hadn't even batted an eyelash at learning the wedding had been called off. They simply waved them on and took up the reins to deal with the chaos Tessa was leaving behind.

That's what they did. They had each other's back. No questions asked.

He just hadn't thought everything through—like the fact she'd come home with him.

She doesn't want to be alone right now, he reminded himself as he stepped out into the hall. That reminder had been the only thing that had kept him from snapping. He wasn't used to sharing his space. Three days of it was about as much as he could handle.

The glorious scent only intensified as he headed for the kitchen.

He *really* needed her to stop baking. He had an upcoming fight, and he didn't need to be worrying about cutting weight because of his sister's broken heart. All the same, he grabbed one of the chocolate chip cookies sitting on a plate on the counter and shoved it into his mouth as he leaned against the doorway to the kitchen. Princess, his white Persian cat, trotted in from the living room and pressed her side into his leg. He lifted her up and scratched her underneath the chin. Purrs vibrated through her small body.

Other than a quick glance and a tight smile, Tessa didn't acknowledge him.

She hadn't looked good since he'd opened his door to find her crying. Eyes constantly swollen and bloodshot. Shoulders drooped in sadness. This morning was no different. She had her blond hair pulled up in a haphazard ponytail. There were chocolate stains on her pale yellow T-shirt. This was so not his usually pristine sister.

His chest hurt for her. He couldn't imagine having to

make a decision like she had, loving someone with all your heart, but both wanting different futures. It seemed like an impossible situation to try to get through.

"Nick call?" he asked around a mouthful of sweet chocolate goodness as he lowered Princess to the floor. She ran over to her bowl, which now sat beside the metal domed trash can.

Moved again.

"Four times already this morning," she said, without looking up. She opened the oven door and withdrew the brownies. Immediately, his mouth begged for a taste.

Sweet Jesus, he was going to gain twenty pounds before she left. He walked over to the trash can and picked up Princess's bowls. After giving her fresh water in one, he filled the other with her favorite wet cat food then put them back down where he'd originally had them—outside the kitchen, underneath the bar.

As he straightened, Tessa tossed her cooking mitts on the counter and turned to face him. Exhaustion creased her face. She loved Nick, deeply. Unfortunately, deal breakers were deal breakers.

Not having kids would've been his, too.

"I took the chicken-shit way out, Brody."

Maybe outsiders would see it that way. But he didn't. He saw it as trying to survive a bad situation. "Let me ask you one question. If, instead of just up and leaving, you'd told him you were thinking about calling off the wedding because of the kid thing, how would this have ended?"

A defeated sigh blew out of her. "He would've talked me into staying, and I would've married him."

"Then you did what *you* had to do. That's all I care about."

She rubbed her forehead with the tips of her fingers. "It hurts so damn bad."

"You love him, sis. No one's questioning that."

She sent him a sad smile. "I know." She paused for a moment. "Everyone will be home today. I'm going to let you go back to your bachelor ways and stay with Savannah until I can find a place to live."

"Well, that household will keep you busy."

Savannah was the oldest. She was happily married, with three beautiful girls under the age of five. He had a special relationship with her oldest daughter, Ellie, who had named his cat. Tessa would be much happier over there than she would be here. The kids alone would make her really smile.

But his family wouldn't be the only people returning to town today.

Scarlett would be, too.

Tessa hadn't been the only one who'd taken the chicken-shit way out. As soon as he'd had an escape, he'd snatched it, leaving Scarlett with only a quick note. But he couldn't spend another three days on that island with her. The kiss had been a mistake. Not only did he feel like he'd taken advantage of a woman in pain, he'd now kissed his best friend's wife and might have mucked up any possibility of them getting back together.

He'd seen with his own two eyes that she wasn't rational right now. She was aiming to hurt Ryan the same way he'd hurt her...and Brody refused to be the way she did it. He might be furious with Ryan over the possibility he'd used Brody as a smokescreen to cheat on his wife, but at the same time, he wanted to stay out of the drama.

Which was why he was going to talk to Ryan today. Clear the air.

"You going to be okay?" he asked.

A slight shrug lifted her shoulder. "Not right now, but I will be. With the pressure of the wedding off, I need to talk to Nick and end things properly. He'll go back to New York. I'll move back here...start over. It's going to be hard. But I have you guys."

So, Tessa had firmly made her decision. She and Nick were over.

Pulling her to his side, he kissed the top of her head and squeezed her. "You'll always have us." He released her. "I have shit-ton of things to do, so I'll be out most the day."

Dealing with Ryan. Confronting his coach. If things went badly there, the day was going to be a fucking long one.

"I'll probably be gone when you get back. Savannah's coming straight from the airport to pick me up."

"I'm only a phone call away," he said.

"I know, big brother."

A little reluctantly, he left. Twenty minutes later, he parked his Mercedes in front of the taupe, stacked-stoned, two-story house—what used to be Ryan and Scarlett's home. Hesitation crept in. How was Ryan going to react?

If it were him, estranged or not, the idea of his best friend being with his wife would enrage him. There were some lines a friend shouldn't cross. Hooking up with your boy's ex was one of them.

He just needed to get it done, face the consequences, whatever they may be.

After walking up the small cement path that led to the two-step porch, he rang the doorbell. Nervous energy knotted his insides. He wasn't usually affected by anxiety, but he was having a serious case of it right now.

A second later, Ryan answered, surprise evident on his face.

"Brody." He opened the door wider, allowing Brody inside. "I wasn't expecting to see you."

"Yeah. Sorry to drop in on you like this, but we have some things we need to talk about."

Ryan ran a palm over his face. He looked just as haggard as Tessa had. "Yeah. I guess we do. Have a seat." He gestured to the chocolate-colored leather couch.

After Brody sat, an awkward silence fell around them. Something new. They were never awkward around each other.

"So…how was the wedding?" Ryan asked.

Chitchat probably wasn't appropriate at the moment, but it was better than just coming out and saying, "Hey. I kissed your wife." Hell, he wasn't even sure how he was supposed to broach a subject like that.

"It didn't happen. Tessa bailed."

"Whoa. Why?"

"After a few drinks, her fiancé let her know he didn't want to have kids."

Pressing his lips together, Ryan slowly nodded. "I can see how that's a problem."

"I'm just glad it came out before they got married."

"Yeah, that was nice." Ryan stared over Brody's shoulder. "They can have a clean break without things getting complicated." He ran his palm over his face again then shook his head.

Brody studied his friend of almost twenty-two years. They'd been inseparable since they were on the same little league team. He knew Ryan almost as well as he knew himself—or at least, he thought he had. Now, he wasn't so sure. But he did know his friend's mannerisms. The man was being eaten up alive by something.

Was it Scarlett? Did he regret his behavior? Wanted her back? The man definitely was a fool for jeopardizing his relationship with Scarlett, but Ryan had never been a moron. Scarlett was a good woman, a loving wife—maybe the fool was remembering that.

His friend worked his neck back and forth. "I know you heard Monica in the background that night you called, and that's why you hung up."

Or was it simply guilt that Brody had found out about the

cheating by accident?

Brody shifted on the couch. "Yeah."

"I left Scarlett." He gave a rough laugh. "Or maybe she left me. She found out about the affair. Flipped her fucking shit. Stormed out of here, and I haven't talked to her since."

Affair. A rock formed in Brody's stomach. That didn't sound like a momentary distraction with a new shiny toy. It sounded long term. Maybe Ryan *was* a moron. "How long?"

"What? Me and Monica? A little over a year."

Stunned, Brody rubbed his mouth, trying to pinpoint one topic to concentrate on now that his mind was bombarding him with a thousand different thoughts. "Over a year? How often did you use me to go see your side piece?"

Ryan's eyes narrowed into thin slits. "Monica is *not* my side piece. Don't *ever* call her that again."

The anger in his friend's voice took Brody aback. He was defending the woman he cheated with? The relationship must be a hell of a lot deeper than superficial, then.

"To answer the question, though, I *never* used you. I know how you feel about cheating, and I'd never bring you into something you are vehemently against. When I told Scarlett I was with you, I was. Period. To see Monica, I used work and business trips."

Brody believed him. A slight weight lifted, knowing that he hadn't been used to hurt Scarlett without his knowledge.

"Anyway," Ryan continued, "I was going to finally come clean to Scarlett, but she found out before I could tell her."

Seemed like he'd had plenty of opportunity to "come clean" over the last year. Goddamn. He couldn't understand how his friend could lie to his wife for that long. "Why didn't you tell Scarlett the moment it happened?"

"I don't know. The first time just happened. Scarlett and I had been having issues for a while. I met Monica at a bar one night. That was the best fucking I'd had in eight years."

Brody recoiled from Ryan's words. *Eight years.* That was exactly how long he'd been with Scarlett.

"I felt so much better afterward," he continued. "Thought maybe a little side fling was what I needed to let loose of the anger I felt when I was around Scarlett. And it worked. I didn't find myself so annoyed with her and her mood swings. I was more patient."

That was news to him. Ryan had been angry at Scarlett? "What was Scarlett moody about?"

Ryan's gaze latched on to his before he glanced away again. "Everyday shit, bro. She couldn't handle stress anymore. Cried over anything. Became volatile and confrontational. Nothing I did was good enough. Our life wasn't good enough. She wanted more than I could give."

That didn't sound anything like the Scarlett he knew. She was a rather easygoing woman. She didn't need extravagance. But he didn't live with her. "What couldn't you give her?"

Again his gaze flicked up to his. "That's her issue. Not mine."

The response didn't surprise Brody. If his friend had one flaw, it was his need to keep up the golden-boy appearance, which was obviously why he'd never confided in Brody about the affair. If he had any fault in "Scarlett's issue" which had caused problems with their marriage, he wouldn't own up to it. In his mind, everything was in Scarlett's head.

"When did things become regular with Monica?"

He remained silent for a moment. "I couldn't get her out of my mind. She'd slipped me her number, and before I even really understood what I was doing, I called her. What was nothing more than a stress-relieving booty call on both our parts slowly turned into more."

"Why did you wait? Why did you let Scarlett find out?"

"Dude, I just told you." He poked his temple with his finger. "She's messed up in the head. I was worried that leaving her would completely destroy her."

"You think letting her find out on her own was better?"

"Whose fucking side are you on, bro?" Ryan scowled at him. "Yeah, what I did wasn't right, but you have no idea what it's like to be married to a frigid, emotionally unstable woman."

As a red haze curtained his vision, Brody cracked his knuckles. "That's your wife you're talking about, Ryan. You took fucking vows. I know Scarlett, too. I know how level-headed she usually is. A woman like that doesn't become emotionally unstable for no damn reason. What was really going on?"

Ryan's jaw clenched. "Are you asking if I did something to her?"

"Well, you did. You cheated on her."

"When did you become the moral police?"

"Since I held your wife while she sobbed because of you."

Ryan's mouth snapped shut and he blinked. "What the hell are you talking about?"

"Scarlett was in the Bahamas. *She* is the reason I called you that night."

"She was in the Bahamas?" He cupped the back of his head with a stunned expression. "That's so...un-Scarlett-like."

"She was doing a lot of un-Scarlett-like things."

Interest piqued on Ryan's face. "Really? Good for her."

Brody shook his head. *Good for her*?

He was having a hard time grasping the man sitting in front of him. For the last year, Ryan had led him to believe everything was hunky-dory in his marriage. That they were always going on trips, enjoying each other. "You didn't go to the mountains with Scarlett a few weeks ago, did you?"

Ryan sat a little straighter and pressed his lips together. "No."

"All this happy-in-love shit you've been spouting off to

me the last few months was never about Scarlett."

"No. I'm in love with Monica. I finally found someone I'm completely compatible with. Thank God. I was sick of trying to get Scarlett to try new things."

"I can't see anyone not wanting to go and do new things, Ryan."

"In bed, bro. I can't even get her to say the word cock. No man should have to deal with that. I don't know how many times I told her to loosen the hell up."

Brody clenched his hands into tight fists. "You critiqued your wife's lovemaking skills?"

"Who's talking about lovemaking? I'm talking about fucking. We might be married, but I still want to fuck. Scarlett doesn't know how to fuck. She's too uptight. Too embarrassed. Timid. It was cute at first, but Jesus Christ, after eight years, learn to give some head. Watch a video... Something."

Unable to listen to another word, Brody shot off the couch. Ryan jerked back. "Dude, what's up your ass?"

Rage shook his entire body as he snatched his ex-best friend by the collar of his shirt. "You're a piece of shit."

His eyes went wide, and he latched his hand on Brody's wrist. "You've lost your goddamn mind. Let me go."

"You're the reason she's so uncomfortable in her own skin. You're the reason she doubts her sexual appeal. No woman should ever have to deal with that, *especially* from her husband."

"Dude, it's not my fucking fault she's frigid."

Brody gave a short jab, popping Ryan in the mouth. His head jerked back. Blood seeped from the crack in his lip. Brody shoved him onto the couch and pointed at him. "Stay the fuck away from, Scarlett. As for us, our friendship is over. I don't associate with people who treat women like dirt."

He strode straight through the front door and slammed it behind him. His body still shook from suppressed fury. A spouse's duty was to build their significant other up, not tear them down. The world did that enough—a person shouldn't have to come home to more of it.

Goddamn it.

Scarlett had never been treated the way she needed. He'd felt her in his arms, responding to his kiss, his touches, and she was brimming with desire. That louse in there just didn't know how to bring it out.

Brody brought it out in her. Easily.

And he planned to continue doing so.

• • •

"You're being selfish, Scarlett."

Closing her eyes, Scarlett tightened her grip on the edge of the sink, and she silently counted to ten before she completely lost it on her mother and sister. She hadn't even been back in town an hour before they'd tracked her down at Delaney's. Seemed they had stopped by to see her at home, and Ryan had let them know she'd left him. It didn't take any genius for them to figure out where she'd gone.

Ten minutes ago, they'd showed up unannounced.

As soon as Delaney had seen who was at the door, she'd made an excuse about needing to get some work done and bolted. Her best friend was not a fan of Scarlett's family. Words had been exchanged before, so Scarlett was glad that she'd made herself scarce.

Too much drama was going on right now, anyway. She didn't need any more.

"Look at me," her mother demanded.

Letting out a slow breath, she faced Mommy Dearest, who sat at the scarred wood kitchen table beside Scarlett's younger sister, Dorothy. Back when her mother still had a personality, she'd named her daughters after her favorite classic movie heroines. But that was before.

Now her mother was bitter and shrill. Though, looking at her, most would only see an ultra-conservative, middle-aged woman. Scarlett knew better.

"You have to go back to him," her mother stated frankly, as she placed her coffee cup on the kitchen table then brushed a lock of dyed blond hair behind her ear. "Divorce is unacceptable, Scarlett. We don't divorce in this family."

No. They just stayed in miserable marriages.

Her parents had been married for thirty-five years, and neither could stand to be in the same room with the other. Scarlett could remember a time when her parents had been happy. Where they had laughed and acted like a true family—supportive and caring.

She'd been eleven. Dorothy had been eight.

Everything changed after her father had lost his job. He couldn't find a new one. He'd gotten a little too heavy with the drink and had a one-night stand with a waitress. Unlike Scarlett's lousy husband, her dad had been riddled with guilt and confessed the morning after it happened.

After that, her once loving, fun-filled mother slowly became spiteful, distrustful, and full of anger. Many times Scarlett wondered if her mother had just ended the marriage, healed, and moved on, then would the woman she remembered from her early childhood have returned.

Now the bitterness was so ingrained in her that the caring mother she'd once been would never be seen again.

Through it all, though, Dad had never left her. When she was older, he admitted that he felt like it was his punishment for messing up. Guilt had kept him married to a woman who hated him until he'd passed away a couple of years ago—a different generation's way of thinking which she couldn't wrap her mind around.

"Well, I believe in divorce," she said and rubbed her

aching forehead. She'd known dealing with her family was going to blow, but she thought she'd have a little more than an hour before having to listen to their harping.

"It's your fault, you know," Dorothy piped in. What she thought she knew about relationships was beyond Scarlett. Her sister hadn't been with a guy longer than six months. "You made this happen. All you've done is nag that man for years. No wonder he turned to another woman."

Hurt by her sister's words, Scarlett swallowed. Not that she'd expected any support from them. Everything was always her fault. This time was no different. Heaven forbid Ryan be held accountable for the fact he couldn't keep his junk in his pants. Nope, it had to be her attitude that forced him to cave to temptation.

"From what I understand, a marriage takes two people. I didn't stray from our marriage, he did."

Her mother shook her head and made a tsking sound, clearly disagreeing with her statement. "Maybe if you'd let the baby nonsense go, none of this would've happened."

Scarlett couldn't stop a shocked gasp of pain, and she had to look away to get control of her emotions. She couldn't believe her mother had just gone there. Never, ever should she have told them about her infertility. Delaney had listened but didn't really understand, since she was nowhere near ready for children. She'd thought this would be one topic she could actually get some support on.

She'd been wrong, and it had been the last thing she'd confided to her mother and sister.

The shit storm from everyone—her mom, her sister… from Ryan for sharing their business—had taught her to keep her mouth shut. All that mattered were appearances.

"Ryan and I started that journey together, remember? We were both on board."

And full of hope. Their marriage was never perfect by

any means, but dreams of children were something they'd shared. After they tried for a year without success, they started seeking help. Two failed IVFs later, the verdict was in. Their inability to have a baby was her fault. Chromosomal abnormities of the eggs—i.e., her eggs sucked.

And Ryan changed.

"When he refused any other option, you should've let it be," her sister said. "But you didn't. You had to stay on him, and when he still refused, all you did was cry about it."

Because at first she thought it was just shock, but as the wedge between them grew wider, and his attitude toward her became more critical, she had to accept that Ryan was never going to use a donor or adopt. And then she'd grieved for the children she would never have.

Because her family didn't divorce. They stuck it out.

She should've left two years ago when Ryan made that decision, but she'd thought they'd get through it. Just a hump in their marriage.

Yeah. So much so, he'd gotten another woman pregnant.

"Listen, I don't need your approval. I left him, that's all you need to know."

"Now you have to go back to him," her mother stated firmly.

Scarlett slammed her palms down on the table. "Are you fucking listen to me?"

Both their eyes widened as they sat up straighter, almost in unison.

"*He* cheated on me. I'm divorcing his sorry ass, going to find myself again, and live a goddamn happy life. Do you hear me?"

Her mother laid her hand on her heart, her mouth moving as if she wanted to say something. Finally, she managed to speak through her indignation. "That man has taken care of you. Paid for your college. Put a roof over your head. So he had a little fling. Get over it and stop being an ungrateful brat."

Scarlett lifted her chin and stared down at her mother. "Maybe I'm being a brat, but I refuse to become a cold-hearted bitch like you."

Her mother's pained, "How dare you," gave her little satisfaction. But the woman deserved a slap back for the years of non-support.

"That wasn't cool, Scarlett," Dorothy said.

"Yeah? Well, the truth hurts."

Her mother shoved back her chair. "I'm not going to sit here and listen to this."

Good. Maybe her family would finally stay out of her business. She was never going to get the support she craved from them. They were two peas in a pod, and she hated that her mother's attitude had rubbed off on her sister. Dorothy would make the perfect, docile wife one day.

Her mother headed for the kitchen door, then she stopped and turned around. "You took vows before God. I don't care what was done to you, to me—you don't break those vows."

At the reprimand, Scarlett swallowed. She'd thought that way once. Had put up with more than she should have because of that strong belief. And it had killed a little part of her. Though the pregnancy hurt tremendously, Ryan had set her free. "I know what you think, Mom. And I respect that. That was your choice to make. This is my choice. And you need to respect that."

"I can't respect someone who gives up."

"Okay, then. You know the way out."

As her mother and sister filed from the room, she shook her head. Her mother would never see Scarlett's divorce as anything but a failure of her own making.

Tears pricked the back of her eyes, but she refused to cry anymore. She was done trying to please other people.

She'd spent her life doing just that. If it wasn't her mother, it was Ryan—trying so damn desperately to be everything he wanted, especially in the last couple of years as he critiqued her relentlessly. She tried, and it was never enough, so she tried harder. What had that commitment gotten her?

A husband who'd sought a good lay to replace the shitty one he was getting at home.

Never again would she put her happiness behind someone else's.

Never.

. . .

Why had she opened the damn door without checking first?

Her heart hadn't even had time to recover from the confrontation with her mother and sister. They'd barely been gone an hour.

Now the blasted organ was going crazy again, but this time the increased beats weren't caused by anger. The acceleration was due to the man standing in front of her—the man who'd left an entire island to get away from her, and who looked devilishly handsome in his training shorts and red shirt, with a lock of dark hair falling across his forehead. She crossed her arms and pursed her lips. "How did you find me?"

He shrugged. "Process of elimination."

"How do you know where Delaney lives?"

"Remember that time we were getting coffee and Delaney called you?"

"Ahh. Yeah. You dropped me off here." That seemed like a lifetime ago. Back when they could hang out without some crazy attraction taking over. Before he got too busy to hang out with her. "I forgot about that."

When she didn't make a move to let him in, he finally asked, "Can I come in? I'd like to talk."

She didn't budge. After dealing with her mom and sister, she really wasn't in the mood to deal with Brody and his loyalty to her ex-husband.

"Scarlett, please. I don't like how we left things in the Bahamas."

She didn't, either. Sighing, she dropped her arms and stepped back, allowing him room to come inside. "Delaney's out taking photos."

"That's good. I'd rather talk to you alone, anyway."

While he paced from one side of the small living room to the other, she sat down on the couch. He seemed nervous, but Brody wasn't the nervous type. "What's on your mind?"

Stopping, he studied her with those amazing brown eyes, then waved between the two of them. "This thing between us. That didn't just manifest for you because of where we were, did it?"

"I'm not sure what you're asking."

"You know…you were on a romantic island, anyone can get caught up in the moment… Is that what happened with you?"

This was not the "talk" she'd expected, which had been more of a lecture on why nothing could ever happen between them, or how much he regretted their kiss. He could still be heading in that direction, and she could save some serious face by saying she *had* gotten caught up in the moment.

"No." Why lie about how she felt? It never helped anything. "What happened in the Bahamas wouldn't have happened if I didn't feel the attraction."

"Yeah. Thought so." He cleared his throat. "Why don't we give it a shot?"

Scarlett jerked back. Now, *that* was really unexpected. "What happened between then and now that made you change your mind? You made it pretty clear Ryan's friendship meant more to you than a fling with me."

Grimacing, he rubbed the back of his head. "I've had time to think. You're no longer with Ryan. Ryan's with someone else. So, why not?"

Why not?

One, she wasn't interested in getting involved with anyone right now. Two, though she couldn't deny the attraction she had to Brody, that was a whole can of worms she wasn't sure she was ready to deal with.

She guessed this was her first chance at doing what made her happy. So she needed to be clearer on what Brody was hinting at.

"When you say, 'give it a shot,' what exactly do you mean?"

"Date. See where things go."

She'd made a promise to herself that she was done making other people happy—she was going to do what made *her* happy. And right here was the perfect opportunity to start putting herself first.

"Let me stop you right now." She held up her hand as she came to her feet. "I just got out of an eight year marriage, and I'm not looking to get into another one. To be perfectly blunt, I have zero interest in getting into another committed relationship. Ever."

"You can't possibly mean that, Scarlett."

"Oh, I do. So, before we go any further in this discussion, we need to be clear on that. This won't be a situation where we see"—she used air quotes—"where things go."

His jaw tightened. "What kind of situation will it be, then?"

Warmth crept up her neck and into her cheeks. She cursed the reaction. She could be sensual and sexy. Damn it. "We take pleasure from each other."

Amusement kicked up one corner of his mouth, and another rush of heat flamed her face.

"What kind of pleasure, Scarlett?"

There wasn't anything condescending or impatient in his tone. Even though she knew Brody found her attempts humorous, she wasn't embarrassed. She felt challenged, and she embraced it.

Racking her brain, she tried to find the words she wanted to use. Many came to mind, but the idea of actually vocalizing them caused her skin to scorch.

Why was it so hard?

Naughty talk was supposed to be easy between two adults who found each other attractive, but she couldn't force the words out of her mouth.

Brody strode straight toward her and stopped barely an inch away. It suddenly became difficult to draw in a breath. He was so overwhelming—the way she had to tilt her head back to look up at him, the power of his body so close to hers... Her nipples puckered into hard peaks.

He ran the back of two fingers down her cheek. "Just say what you want."

Swallowing first, she opened her mouth. And again, nothing came out.

The heated way he held her gaze made her feel exposed.

Leaning forward, he brushed his lips across the outer curve of her ear as he whispered huskily, "Fuck, Scarlett. You want to fuck."

An excited shiver raced over her. She'd hated that word before, thought it was trashy, but coming out of Brody's mouth it was exotic.

"Say it," he softly demanded, his lips continuing to tease her ear.

A stuttered breath shot out of her mouth, then she murmured, "I want to fuck."

Saying the word aloud in a purely sexual way didn't make her feel trashy. It made her feel empowered. She'd finally said what she wanted.

Brody lifted his head, his mouth inches from her. She couldn't look away from him; he had her snared, ready to follow wherever he planned to take her. And she had no doubt that Brody would take her to a place she'd never been before, an exciting place she might never want to come back from.

"Never filter yourself during sex."

Then he backed away. Instantly, she missed the heat of his large body.

Seriousness encased his chiseled face, and she realized the moment was over. He was back to business. How was he able to turn it off and on like that? She felt like a basket of exposed nerves.

"So, that's what you're looking for?" he asked. "A fuck buddy?"

She cringed away from the simplification of her desires, and he apparently noticed, because he added, "Don't be ashamed of what you want. There's nothing wrong with just wanting to enjoy sex with no strings attached. I, on the other hand, will have some rules if this is the arrangement we agree upon."

He was right. There was nothing wrong with her wanting to enjoy a person in her bed. Someone who brought her body to life, who would take the stigma of being frigid off her mind and make her feel like she was a desirable, *fuckable* woman.

"Rules? I didn't think Brody Minton had rules."

"When it comes to my bed partners, I do. I don't fuck around."

Intrigued, she tilted her head to the side. "I assumed you have a long line of women wanting to warm your bed."

"I do," he said, shrugging, but there was no ego in his voice, just a matter of fact truth. "Doesn't mean I have any interest in a different woman warming my sheets every night.

I don't work like that."

"How do you work?"

"When I find a woman I want to take to my bed, it's more than just once, and I don't share. If we're fucking, we're only fucking each other."

She furrowed her brows. "Isn't that being in a relationship?"

"A physical one, yes. That's my rule. If you have no interest in an emotional relationship, but are still curious about exploring this attraction between us, I can respect that. But while we are playing with each other's bodies, *I'll* be the only man you're playing with. Is that acceptable?"

For a long moment, she studied him. She had never made this kind of agreement before. It was like she was making a business deal, but at the same time, she knew Brody was dead serious and wanted to make sure she understood *his* limitation.

"How does an arrangement like this work? Do I just call you when I'm in the mood? Like a booty call?"

As much as she wanted to not get into a relationship, she hated the idea of being someone's booty call.

"No." He sharply shook his head. "I don't do booty calls, either. A woman should be treated with respect and not just called up when I'm in the mood to fuck, or visa versa. We go out, have fun together, then we end the night in bed."

"I don't get it, Brody. That's dating."

"No. We are both aware of each other's agenda. We both know there'll be an expiration date, a time when we're ready to move on. Are you ready to have an *adult* relationship?"

She chewed on her lower lip. He was giving her exactly what she wanted, with no fear of things getting weird between them over unwanted emotions. Just two adults, going in with their eyes wide-open, appreciating each other in a way she'd never truly enjoyed the opposite sex.

"I am."

He nodded once. "I'll pick you up tonight at seven. Be ready."

With that, he left. No good-bye. No kiss. Nothing intimate.

She stared at the closed door.

No pressure.

This might be the best arrangement she'd ever made.

. . .

Brody slammed the door of his car then scrubbed his hands over his face, groaning.

What had he just done?

Made a deal that was doomed to fail, that's what.

He'd come over here certain he was starting the first day of a real relationship with Scarlett. Something he'd once believed would never happen. Ryan had always stood in his way.

Now it looked like Scarlett was the obstacle.

She had no intention of getting into a relationship again. Though in hindsight, he should've considered this possibility. She hadn't just gotten out of a long-term relationship—she'd just ended her marriage, which wasn't even final yet.

He had to respect her decision. The problem was, could he?

He wasn't stupid. Until an hour ago, Scarlett had been forbidden to him. With the dissolving of his friendship to Ryan, and knowing the extent to which the man had hurt Scarlett, he could pursue her in the way he'd only fantasized about. But that idea had been stopped in its tracks.

The moment she'd said she wasn't looking for anything real, he should've walked away. He was already in too deep for this to end any way but badly. Yet, the idea of another man walking into her life and doing all the things he wanted—had always wanted—to do to her forced him to make the damn arrangement.

Now it was his job to keep his own wants under control. She had set the parameters. It wasn't the first time he'd had a relationship based strictly on a physical connection. So this wasn't new. He knew how to do this. He had to stay focused on her pleasure, help her become confident with her body— with her words.

That was the important thing, and no other man would show her that but him.

He cranked the car and drove off. Goddamn, this had already been a fucked up day. And the day wasn't over yet. Next, he had to confront Greg. No more pussy-footing around. It was time to get real with his coach.

He backed out of the driveway, and fifteen minutes later, he strode into Greg's gym. As usual, his coach was standing outside the ring, shouting instructions to his new toy as he sparred with a partner.

Brody approached him then tapped Greg on the shoulder.

He sent Brody a quick glance. "Minton," he said, with a short nod of acknowledgement.

"I need a few minutes with you."

His coach hung his head for a moment. "I don't have time. I'm working with Randy."

Irritation flared hot, and Brody fisted his hands. "Make time," he said between clenched teeth.

Greg turned his head, his gaze traveling over Brody. He pressed his lips in a tight line. As he returned his attention to the ring, he said, "Randy. Take five."

Five minutes was all the time Greg was going to give him. Well, if that didn't feel like a kick to the goddamn gut.

"What's eating at you, Minton?"

The glances he was getting from the other fighters were making him uncomfortable. "Privacy would be nice."

Greg blew out an annoyed breath. "Come on, then."

The jerk was making the decision a lot easier on Brody. They had a long past. He'd thought they could sit down, hash out their differences, and things would get better. Greg's current attitude only confirmed what Brody had always known.

He was done.

As Greg sat down in his chair, he leveled Brody with an impassive stare. "What?"

"It's time we parted ways."

He didn't know what he expected from his coach. A little shock maybe. Some hesitation. But a quick, "You're right," left Brody fumbling for his footing.

"It's something I've been thinking long and hard on, too," Greg continued. "I don't have anything more to offer you, Minton. You've been a part of this gym for years. I've invested a lot of time into you, and you haven't produced the results I expected by now. I've had to accept you just don't have that 'it' factor I'm looking for."

Greg's words fed the thoughts Brody had been having ever since those articles had come out, and it only succeeded in pissing him off even more. "Fuck you, Greg. I bust my ass in here training. You've never gotten less than one-hundred percent of me in the cage."

"And yet, you still haven't been good enough to get out of the middle of the pack and really shine. I can only do so much. You've had a great career, Minton. Made some great money. Be proud of that. But it's time for me to put all my focus on Randy, who *does* have the 'it' factor."

His body shook from trying to restrain his anger. "Maybe it has nothing to do with me. Maybe it's the coach. Ever thought of that? The only titled fighter you've had under this roof was Richard Sentori, but he had a belt when he came here, didn't he? What happened when he took you on as his coach?"

Red crept up the man's neck and into his cheeks as his nostrils flared. "Get the fuck out of here, Minton."

"Gladly. I'll go find me a coach who actually helps make winners, you fucking asshole."

Brody spun and stormed past the fighters, who'd undoubtedly heard the entire exchange, if their slacked-jawed expressions were anything to go by. Embarrassment rushed over him, infuriating him more. He despised creating a public spectacle. He'd let his anger get the better of him, and he'd willingly participated in this one. *And* they'd heard his coach all but call him a has-been.

Fuck him and fuck this. He had the ability to be the heavyweight champion, and he was going to prove that it was the coaching keeping him from advancing, and not the fighter. There was only one person he could think of that he'd want in his corner.

Mike Cannon.

After jumping into his car and racing across town, he stopped in front of Mike's facility. Tightening his grip on the steering wheel, he pushed out a long breath then climbed out. He had to go in there calm and collected, and not like some enraged fighter fueled off emotions. Mike didn't respond to stuff like that.

He stepped into the facility and scanned the interior. The training center was larger than Greg's. But the two biggest differences were the fighter sparring with a trainer inside the traditional boxing ring, and the other fighter grappling on blue mat—the two titleholders. Dante "Inferno" Jones and Tommy "Lightning" Sparks.

Mike trained champions. Greg put all his energy into maybes. *Fuck*. Was a maybe all he was?

The unwanted thought hit him with the power of a punch on the sweet spot, wiping away the confidence he'd felt as he stormed out of Greg's gym. What if he was wrong and Greg and the news articles were right?

He didn't have time to dwell on it as the bald and muscular owner strode out of a back office. Nervous energy zapped through Brody. Seemed "nerves" was the word of the day. That was the third time he'd been afflicted with the shit.

Big day of changes with unexpected outcomes, he supposed.

As much as he wanted Mike as his coach, it was very possible the man would tell him no. He had the reputation of being extremely choosey about who he trained. Hell, he'd even cut ties with two title holders, Richard Sentori and Tommy, because of their behavior.

After being defeated by Dante, Sentori went on to fall flat on his face with Greg as his coach. He was no longer in the CMC and was now fighting for lesser-known MMA organizations, while Tommy had made a huge comeback that Mike respected, and so had allowed him back on his roster.

Mike didn't fuck around.

"Brody." The beefy man walked over to him and extended his hand, which Brody took firmly. "What brings you to this side of town?"

"I was hoping we could talk."

Mike's brows arched up, indicting his surprise. "I'm intrigued. Come on. Let's talk in my office."

He followed the other man into a small office. Mike sat behind a desk, and Brody took a seat in a beat-up old leather chair. Mike leaned back and hooked his arms behind his head. "What can I do for you?"

And here went nothing. "Do you have room in your house for a new fighter?"

Mike studied him for a long moment. The silence only increased the nerves churning in his stomach. He wanted this…bad.

"Why do you want to leave Greg?" Mike finally asked.

No reason to sugarcoat anything. The entire facility had heard the exchange between them. It would be the talk of every locker room across the country by tomorrow. "Greg and I have outgrown each other."

"You outgrew each other, or are you butt-sore over him focusing on Randy Boss?"

At Mike's bluntness, Brody blinked, having a hard time finding the right words to answer the question. He finally settled on, "Both."

"I'm not going to blame Greg for putting his energy into Randy. From what I've heard, CMC is impressed with him, and think he's going to have a huge career. I've also heard that you're reaching the end of yours. What do you think I could do for you that Greg hasn't?"

Palms sweating, Brody rubbed his hands over his fighting shorts. "I've been with Greg for a long time. I need a change. A new direction with my training. You can do that for me."

Mike picked up a pen and started jotting something down on a yellow legal notebook. "I don't ego stroke, Minton. I'm sure you've heard that about me," he said, without looking up. "I haven't been impressed with your last two appearances in the cage. You're scheduled to fight Raster in a few weeks, and we both know that's a step back for you."

Not that he was surprised by Mike's knowledge of the goings-on in the MMA world, but he was surprised that Mike was aware of Brody's schedule when his opponent wasn't part of this gym.

"Yeah. It is."

"So, why should I sign a fighter whose career is going backward and not forward?"

Fucking ouch. Not only had he been verbally bitch-smacked by his ex-coach, Mike was adding insult to injury. Brody squared his shoulders. "Because *I* say I'm not done.

The last thing I need is another fucking coach who has lost his faith in my ability in the cage. If you can't get behind me, then this meeting is over."

Mike glanced up, respect shining in his eyes. "I'll tell you what. I'll coach you for this next fight. Call it a trial run. This'll be a good way for both of us to see if it's the coaching or if it's the fighter that has taken your career in the wrong direction." Mike stood and offered his hand. "Do we have a deal, Minton?"

Mike was offering him a moment of truth. If he lost this next fight, or put in another bad performance ending with a lucky win, he'd have to face some hard facts.

Pushing that thought aside, he stood and took Mike's hand in another firm shake. "Deal."

Now he had to prove himself.

Chapter Seven

Had she made a mistake? Where was Delaney? Scarlett paced the living room.

It'd been almost two hours since Brody had left, and in that time, her insecurities had gone crazy.

Unless things went horribly wrong, she was going to have sex tonight—with Brody. What if she did something stupid? Brody hadn't blinked an eye when she'd ineptly tried to explain what she wanted. Instead, he'd turned the tables and made the moment hotter than anything she'd ever experienced. With only words.

She wasn't such a smooth talker. But talking dirty wasn't her only concern. Trying to get her marriage back on track, she'd experimented with different things, even gone as far as taking a burlesque class. She'd been so proud of herself and had been excited to show her husband what she'd learned.

And he'd laughed. Humiliated, she hadn't finished the routine, and he hadn't encouraged her to continue.

She's stopped trying after that. What if Brody laughed? What if tonight just proved that she sucked in bed? A wave of nausea assaulted her.

Oh God. She couldn't do this.

The front door opened behind her, and she whirled around.

"Thank God!"

Delaney froze just inside the door. "I've been gone a few hours. What the hell could have happened in that amount of time?"

"Lots." Scarlett motioned for to hurry inside.

Delaney closed the door, rushed into the living room, and sat down on the couch. "Spill it."

Where did she even begin? She bit her thumbnail. "Brody left a couple of hours ago."

"Okay," she drawled out the word.

"We made an arrangement."

Delaney cocked her head.

Scarlett inhaled deeply. "We agreed to an adult relationship."

"An adult relationship?" Delaney's face screwed into a what-the-hell expression. "Is that some mature way of saying fuck buddies?"

A laugh shot out of Scarlett mouth. At least Delaney needed a clearer definition, too. "Not according to Brody. His definition of…" She hesitated over the next two words. *Say it, girl.* "Fuck buddies"—she suppressed a grin as satisfaction coursed through her—"means only having sex like a booty call. People in an adult relationship still go out before ending up in bed, and there are no strings attached."

Delaney pursed her lips then shrugged. "Sounds like a sweet deal, Scar. I mean Brody wants to wine and dine you, rock your world, and there's nothing expected. So…hell, yeah."

Scarlett breathed a sigh. She didn't know why it was so important for her to hear that from her friend, but it was. "So you don't think I'm crazy?"

"Hell, no. If there's one person who deserves to have some fun, it's you."

She deserved it, but deep down, the worry about disappointing Brody threatened to ruin that fun. What if Brody called uncle before the end of the night because she was too uptight? Could she recover from the humiliation on top of everything she'd already been through?

"What's got you freaked?"

Good lord, was she wearing "I think I suck" on her forehead? "How can you tell I'm freaked?"

Delaney cocked a brow. "How long have we been friends?"

"Forever."

"Exactly."

Scarlett licked her lips. She hadn't told Delaney everything about her marriage. Some things were just better left unsaid, and if she'd confided in Delaney, her friend would have hated Ryan. Now, it didn't really matter. Besides, maybe her friend could give her some tips.

"How do you please a man?"

"What are you talking about?"

"Like give them unforgettable sex. You said you and Blake had the most amazing sex ever. How?"

Delaney stared wide-eyed at Scarlett. "Have you never had amazing sex, Scar?"

"I don't think so."

"Okay, that's a no," her friend said, shaking her head in disbelief.

"Ryan critiqued me a lot."

"Critiqued you? Like, not in the 'babe, I love it when you do this' way?"

"No, more like, you'll never get me to nut with that kind of blow job."

As the crass words left her mouth, her face heated crimson, but if she was going to be honest, she had to say it exactly how he'd say it.

"That motherfucker." Delaney's jaw clenched. "My guess is he couldn't get your motor revving and wanted to make you feel inadequate instead of accepting responsibility for being a shitty lover."

A small smile came to Scarlett's lips. She could always count on Delaney to make her feel better.

"Listen to me, Scar. Don't let that asshole into your head. Don't let him make you doubt your abilities."

"Unfortunately, he already has. I have so much negativity in my head from sex that I'm scared everything I do is stupid."

"Did you doubt yourself when you were with Brody?"

"That doesn't really count. We never got past kissing. I'm not sure what would've happened if we had."

Delaney studied her for a long moment. "Do you play with the balls when you go down?"

Her face scorched. "I—uh. What?"

Delaney held her hand out, palm up, and slowly wiggled her fingers. "You know, cup them, massage them, kiss them, tongue them."

"Jesus, Delaney."

A brow arched up. "Well?"

"I've never been sure what to do with them."

"Okay." Without another word, she disappeared into her bedroom, returning a few seconds later with one of her thigh high stockings. She walked into the kitchen and grabbed two Cutie tangerines out of a fruit bowl and put them inside the stocking so they hung there…looking very much like a large set of testicles.

Scarlett pressed the back of her hand to her lips, trying to hide her amusement.

"Now," Delaney said, as serious as a schoolteacher, once

she placed her hand underneath the tangerines. "Gently cup them while you're sucking him off. Roll them lightly in your palm. Men love having their balls played with." She held up one finger. "This area here"—she pointed to the crevice where the two tangerines met—"run your tongue over this. Even better. The length of skin between the balls and his asshole, girl...they love having that tongued."

Mesmerized, Scarlett sat down on the couch. "What else?"

"I wish you would've come to me sooner, Scar."

She did, too. If there was anyone in the world she could've been completely open with, it was Delaney. There was no subject—except maybe her ex—that was off-limits. Her friend never would've judged her. Judged Ryan, maybe, but never her.

"How do you talk dirty?"

"I say whatever I want to say." Delaney pursed her lips then came to sit down beside her, taking one of her hands. "Babe, listen. If saying, 'fuck me,' isn't your thing, don't force yourself to do it. Sex is personal. Some things aren't going to be for you, just like something you find you really like might not be for someone else. And *that's* okay. What truly matters is finding a partner who respects your boundaries. I assume Ryan didn't do that."

"Ryan rushed everything. He wanted to try anal. I'd never done it. I wasn't opposed to doing it. I was open to new things. Well—we did it. I saw stars, Delaney, it hurt so bad."

"What he do? Just shove it in?" Scarlett let her expression speak for her, and Delaney grimaced. "Shit, girl. I'd never want to do anal again, either, if I had that happen to me."

"To say the least, I was not as open to doing new positions afterward, which made him angry."

"Did you tell him that he hurt you?"

"I did. He said he'd used a ton of lube like he was supposed to. Then he said if I'd relaxed it wouldn't have hurt as bad."

"It's his responsibility to get you so wound up that you're only thinking about the pleasure he's giving you. Ryan failed. Not you. Don't let his lack of finesse make you put all men in the same category. With the right man, sex is amazing."

"Like it was with Blake?"

Delaney blew out a breath. "Oh, hell yeah. I've had good sex in my lifetime, but that man put them all to shame."

"What was different about him?"

"Let's just say, I knew I was in for a wild ride when he said the safe word was 'black velvet,' and the man didn't disappoint. He met my kinky side one spanking after another."

"You like to be spanked?"

"And choked."

"Choked?"

"You wait. One day you'll have a guy who can make your panties wet just by putting his hand around your throat. No pressure…just by putting it there."

Scarlett did not see that as possible. "I'll just take your word for it."

"I'm just saying, enjoy tonight. Try new things. If you don't like it, that's okay. But you never know what's going to turn you on. Something you never imagined might be the trigger to releasing all this doubt and opening you up to a sexual world that you love."

Delaney was right. Tonight she'd let the past go. Start fresh with a new lover. One who already made her body come to life in a way it never had before, with just a simple touch. She looked forward to what else Brody would do to her tonight.

• • •

She was going to have sex tonight.

Scarlett's stomach clenched as she flicked mascara onto

her lashes. That damn thought had popped up in her head all afternoon. Straightening from the mirror, she thrust the mascara wand back into its tube with more force than necessary then shoved it in her makeup bag. Stepping back, she ran a palm over the cobalt blue fabric of her sundress. The short skirt barely hit mid-thigh. Thin spaghetti straps and low-V neckline showed off shoulders and cleavage. Matching strappy, spiked heels completed the outfit.

Was it too much? She'd tried wearing sexy clothes twice now and had fallen flat on her face both times. Maybe she should've gone with the white baby-doll dress and ballet shoes.

Self-doubt was eating away at her confidence.

"Stop overthinking," Delaney said from Scarlett's bed. "You look petrified. Number one, it's Brody. You know him. You always have fun together. Number two, I know you guys have made this arrangement, but you're putting too much emphasis on the end result. Go into this just wanting to have a good time, and let the rest fall into place."

She looked at Delaney's reflection in the mirror. "Great advice. Got any on how to shut my mind off?"

"Tell it to shut up."

"Easier said than done," she muttered.

The doorbell chimed, and she jumped as Delaney's head snapped toward the door.

"Listen to me," she said hurriedly. "Go with the flow. *No* expectations. *Seriously.* Let the night unfold naturally. If you go into this all freaked out like you are right now, you're going to stress yourself out, and then shit can go bad tonight. Just. Have. Fun."

Scarlett inhaled a deep breath. No expectations. Just have fun.

She could do that.

"Here goes nothing." She strode out her room. Delaney's, "You got this," followed her into the hall. As she made her way to the front door, her heels clacked loudly on the hardwood floor, a reminder that she, alone, would set the tone for tonight. She could either keep with the anxiety, or open that door like a strong, confident woman, ready to face whatever Brody had in store for her.

She chose the latter.

Squaring her shoulders, she opened the door. Air whooshed out of her lungs at the sexy-as-hell man standing on her doorstep in a pair of faded blue jeans that rode low on his hips, and a dark gray T-shirt that strained against his muscular heavyweight build.

Nothing about what he wore said they were heading to anything special.

She'd already made a mistake in this adult relationship thing. She'd treated tonight like a date. She shouldn't have. She should've dressed in her regular clothes and not spent hour agonizing on what to wear.

A wolf whistle caught her off guard, and she jerked her gaze up from his massive chest to his eyes. Blatant hunger stared back at her from their caramel depths. Desire sliced through her, making her nipples bead.

Maybe she hadn't picked the wrong outfit after all.

"Fucking hot," he murmured.

And she stood a little taller, thrusting her breasts out. It was amazing how Brody made her feel like the sexiest woman in the world. Not cute. Not adorable. Not even pretty.

But hot. Sensual. Sexy.

"That makes two of us," she said. "Damn, I'm a lucky girl."

A grin stretched his lips. "You ready?" He held up his hand.

It took her a moment to register the helmet. Then her gaze shot past his shoulder to the road, and her throat tightened. Parked at the curb was Brody's Harley.

She didn't ride. He *knew* that. Had respected that in the

years she'd known him. Why would he bring that damned thing tonight?

"Where's your Mercedes?" she asked, unable to tear her eyes off the death machine.

"At home in the garage."

She finally dragged her gaze to him, only to come face-to-face with his challenging expression. Oh, he could totally go screw himself. "I'm not getting on that thing."

Unlike a lot of women, she'd never had any fantasy about riding a motorcycle. The idea terrified her. Being in a car was unsafe enough, out on the roads with all the crazies, but a two-wheeled out-on-the-open-road bike was suicide. She watched the news.

"Yes, you will," he said, not the slightest bit deterred by her refusal.

"Oh, really?" She crossed her arms, irked by his assurance. "And how exactly do you plan to make me?"

He mimicked her posture. "I'm not going to make you. You're going to do it yourself."

"How's that?"

"Because you want to try new things."

"True. But riding a motorcycle is not on my bucket list. Sorry."

He stepped forward, crowding her into the door. Her heart picked up pace as the scent of his cologne swam around her nose. "Think about it, Scarlett. The vibration between your legs. Your arms wrapped around my waist. The wind whipping past you. No compartment holding you in. You're one with the outdoors. It's a freedom you need to experience at least once."

The image he painted formed in her mind. All she could focus on was his large *body* cradled between her legs as they flew down the highway, her blond hair whipping behind her, her palms pressed to his chest. Why was the idea enticing?

Because it was Brody. Anything with him enticed her.

She couldn't do this, though, for two reasons. One, she couldn't give in that easily. What kind of message was that sending? And two, how could she agree to something she'd never wanted to do, all because he'd said a few perfect words?

She racked her brain for another reason. What if it rained? It'd ruin her hair she'd spent so much time on.

She finally settled on, "I'm not dressed for a bike ride."

"Excuses. Change. Problem fixed." He lowered his head until his lips were just above hers. "Stop fighting it. Come with me, Scarlett."

The innuendo went straight to her clit, making it pulse to life with a demanding ache. Her body wanted what he was saying. *She* wanted it. Was this an adult relationship? Every word a hidden sexual meaning?

She was totally fine with it. She loved this wordplay, hoped she could be a worthy opponent for him. One way to find out.

"Only if you let me ride you first."

She swallowed. That had sounded so damn stupid.

Approval turned up one corner of his lips, though. "You're going to get the ride of your life, darlin'."

A shiver scurried over her. She may be a novice at this sexy talk, but Brody sure wasn't. She looked forward to what he'd say next. Actually looked forward to trying to one-up him with her comebacks.

"I'm holding you to that, buddy," she said, then moved past him and hurried to the back of the house to her bedroom.

As soon as she entered, Delaney's brows furrowed. "Uh, what happened? I couldn't hear anything but your mumbles."

"Brody brought his bike."

A pleased grin came to her friend's face. "Oh, *girrrl*, I love this man. You're going to love it."

Scarlett wasn't as confident.

After changing into a pair of dark jeans and a light

blue and white paisley-printed halter-top, she walked back
to where Brody waited. He let loose another wolf whistle.
Sexy outfit be damned—this man made her feel desirable in
anything she wore.

He opened the front door and gestured for her to go first.
As she passed him, he placed his hand on her lower back,
closed the door behind them, and didn't remove his palm until
they reached his bike. She loved how that made her feel—like
she was special and protected.

As he grabbed an extra helmet, anxiety attacked her
insides. Was she really going to do this?

Brody brushed her hair behind her shoulders, then he
tugged the helmet down over her head. The padding hugged
her cheeks and scalp.

"Ready?"

She glanced at the motorcycle. Honestly, she wasn't sure.
As much as she liked what Brody had said earlier, facing the
reality was a different matter. There was no part of her that
wanted to get on that damn thing.

As if sensing her hesitation, he put on his helmet, straddled
the bike, kicked it to life, then yelled, "Climb on, darlin'."

Yeah, she wanted to climb on—just not the bike. Biting
her lip, she hesitated for a moment longer before hopping on
behind Brody, having to spread her thighs wide to be able to
accommodate his body. As he pulled away from the curb, she
wrapped her arms tight around his waist, noticing immediately
the way the powerful engine vibrated against her.

Oh, this wouldn't be good. Having Brody between her
legs was already turning her on; add a seat vibrator to the
mix, and she was certain to embarrass herself.

Blowing out a breath as Brody sped away from the curb,
she tried to concentrate on the passing scenery, quickly noting
that he wasn't going toward the city, but more out into the
country. The bumpy asphalt was more enjoyable than it

should've been, considering. But every little jostle hit her just right. Lowering her head to the area between his shoulders, she tried to think of anything else, but it was impossible. The longer they rode, the more the seat made her throb, causing her to squirm. As a whimper escaped, she tightened her grip on Brody. She wanted to grind against the seat, anything to relieve the building pressure.

Brody pulled onto a deserted lane then guided the bike behind a line of trees, obscuring the view to the road. After kicking the stand down, he yanked off his helmet and climbed off, leaving the engine idling.

Without a word, he came to stand beside the bike, directly behind her. After removing her helmet, he said, "Lean back."

She shot him a questioning glance, uncertain of what he wanted her to do. He placed a hand on his upper abs. "Here."

Curious, she carefully leaned back so her shoulders were supported by his body. The move caused the crotch of her jeans to move against her clit, and she bit back a moan. After he repositioned her where he wanted her, he flicked open the button of her jeans then lowered the zipper.

"Brody!" She tried to sit up, but his other hand latched onto her shoulder, keeping her in place.

"Shh. You were about to come apart behind me, and I'll be damned if it's the vibration from the engine that gives you the first orgasm of the night."

His hand slipped under her panties and over her slick clit. Groaning, she relaxed into him, widening her legs so he could rub the delicious ache better.

"Damn, woman. You're fucking turned on," he said as he slipped one finger deep inside her.

At the amazing sensations, and the friction of his palm rubbing against her, she closed her eyes, reached behind her, and gripped his biceps, grinding against his hand. Never before had she done something like this. Never out in the open, outside, barely hidden.

The idea of getting caught only fueled her desire. She moved her hips. With the combination of his fingers, the vibration from the engine, and the motion of her hips, she came hard within seconds. Throwing her head back, she moaned her release, her entire body tense.

"That's right. Come for me, darlin.'"

As the orgasm abated, he continued his pressure, pushing her immediately into another climax. When she came down from that one, he slowly removed his hand from her panties.

Slowly, he inserted a glistening finger into his mouth, his eyes locked on hers.

An orgasm wasn't enough. She wanted more. She wanted him pounding into her. From behind. Right here on the dead leaves covering the ground.

"Fuck me, Brody." The words just slipped past her lips without thought.

When she realized what she'd said, her face heated, but she didn't regret the words. Not at all. For the first time, she was completely in the moment. It was all about the way he made her body feel, and she was open to anything as long as these sensations continued.

He fisted his hand in her hair and tugged her head back. Her breathing became choppy as lust flared, white-hot, through her. She loved that he pulled her hair.

Leaning down, he stopped right above her mouth, his breath fanning her face. She could smell herself, and it only increased the hotness of this moment.

"I plan to. Many times." He kissed her lightly, then he straightened and released her. "But not right now. That was for you."

He moved in front of her, tugged his helmet back on, kicked the stand back up, and then turned the cycle around.

Her oversensitive clit ached with the vibration. If the rest of their outing went this way, by night's end, she was going to be a bundle of live nerves.

. . .

Brody could still taste her.

It was an intoxicating flavor, one he couldn't wait to bury his face in and get more of. He revved the engine, speeding up the bike. He'd kept the plans for the night deliberately light — take her outside her comfort zone by getting her on his bike, go for a joy ride, then end up at his condo.

The moment behind the trees had been unexpected and had only encouraged him to cut their trip short and head back to his place — pronto.

Not that Scarlett would mind. Not with her, "Fuck me, Brody."

He'd done that. He'd gotten her so aroused, she'd finally just asked for what she wanted.

By night's end, his plan was to fuck away all the negative thoughts his ex-best friend had put into her head. Ryan didn't deserve any space in her head or her heart. She was the most goddamn beautiful woman he'd ever had the pleasure of watching come. The rock-hard erection he'd gotten just from feeling her squirm behind him had been nothing compared to how hard it had pulsed against his zipper as she'd released. Twice.

He flew down the road. Ten minutes later, he guided the bike into his assigned garage next to his Mercedes. As they rode up in the elevator, tension crept back between them. Scarlett seemed nervous, judging by the way she was picking at her thumbnail with her other one. Doubts had hold of her again. Not good.

He'd seen her walls come down, and he couldn't wait to topple them again. The challenge of taking Scarlett from a nervous, unsure woman to so fucking turned on that she was completely there with him was hot as hell. He got hard as a rock watching the transformation.

He'd allow her the few moments of uncertainty, of overthinking, before he made his move. It wasn't a bad thing for her to have them first, to worry a bit before she saw for herself that it was for nothing.

After he opened the door to his condo, he motioned for her to step inside. She'd been here before, of course, so he didn't expect to do the usual look around that normally happened when he brought someone home. The living room still had the same black leather sofa/love seat combo, the same dark wood coffee tables and end tables, and the same huge picture window looking out over the skyline. Nothing had changed over the past year.

Princess appeared from around a corner and pranced toward them. Scarlett let out a happy squeal. "Oh my God, she's so fluffy."

Except maybe his cat.

Scarlett spun on him with a bright smile. "I knew you'd gotten a Persian, I just couldn't believe it. She's beautiful."

"I'd taken Ellie to the pet store to see the animals."

"Ellie's your niece, right?"

"Yep. We were supposed to only *see* the animals. Instead, I came home with this white ball of fur named—just a bit embarrassingly, I'll admit—by said niece."

"I think it's sweet. Not many uncles would do that, Brody."

"I have a special bond with that child. She was the first baby. I'd spent a lot of time with only her before Savannah had the twins, and they are just now toddling around. It will get really interesting when they get a little older."

Scarlett bent down and picked up Princess, cradling the cat against her chest. She scratched the animal behind the ears. Loud purrs followed.

"She's spoiled rotten," he added with a chuckle.

"I've always wanted a cat," she murmured as she nuzzled the top of Princess's head with her nose.

"I didn't know that. Why haven't you got one?"

A faraway look came to her eyes, then she forced a small smile. "Ryan was allergic."

He wasn't sure if Scarlett was having a momentary lapse of memory or what. But Ryan had been his best friend — that man was no more allergic to cats than he was the air he breathed. But whatever her real reasoning was, she didn't seem ready to share it.

He changed the subject. "Would you like glass of wine?"

He'd specifically bought her favorite merlot this afternoon after leaving Mike's. His smile faded at the passing thought of his new coach. He scrubbed the back of his head.

No heaviness tonight. There would be more than enough time later for him to do his worrying. Mike putting him on a trial run didn't sit well with him. It only added to his own troubled thoughts about where his career was headed.

Scarlett strolled into the living room and sat down with Princess on the couch, cooing, "What a sweet kitty," to the cat.

Enough. He had a woman's insecurities to banish. Those were more important than his at the moment.

After he'd poured them both a glass of wine, he strode to Scarlett, handed her one, then sat down beside her.

Tension immediately stiffened her body as she took a sip from her glass, looking at anything and everything but him.

He could approach this one of two ways. He could simply jump her, get down and dirty, and wipe away her doubt by making her so aroused she couldn't think about anything other than what he was doing to her. *Or* he could push her outside her comfort zone again and make her face her demons head on.

As much as he loved the idea of driving her out of her

mind with his hands, he wanted her to embrace her sexuality more. Which meant they were going to do this slow, but hard—at least, for her.

"How about a game?" he asked.

Her gaze shot to his. "What kind of game?"

There was hesitation in her voice. Man, she was really going to get freaked out. All the more reason to do it. She needed that push. "Truth or Dare. Sex Edition."

Her mouth popped open in the cutest expression of surprise. He wanted to kiss her, but he refrained. She wanted an adult relationship. Now it was time to get very adult with her.

"O-okay," she stammered.

Pride expanded his chest. She hadn't tried to back out. Though she was definitely timid with the idea, she was pushing that aside to try new things.

"I'll go first," he said, not wanting to put her on the spot with the first question. "Truth or Dare?"

"Truth," she said without a moment of hesitation and then downed her glass of wine.

So, she thought truth would be easier than dare? She was wrong.

"What's your favorite position to fuck?" When she started blinking rapidly, he took her glass and went back into the kitchen to refill it, giving her a moment to get her embarrassment under control without him staring at her.

When he walked back into the living room, she locked eyes with him as she said, "Doggie style."

Instantly, an image of her on all fours with him behind her formed in his mind, and his cock stirred. "Why?" There was no denying the husky edge to that one word, and he didn't care one bit.

But she didn't seem to notice, and shook her head. "One question. One answer. My turn. Truth or dare?"

His lips kicked up. He loved that she was jumping into

this. "Truth."

"What do you like having done to you?" she asked, as if she'd had the question prepared for days.

Good question. He sat down beside her and laid his arm across the back of the couch. "That's a given. A blow job."

Pink brightened her cheeks as her gaze slid from his to her hand still stroking his cat. "Yeah, I guess it was a stupid question."

Damn it. The last thing he wanted was for her to start doubting herself. Intensifying her insecurities was not the point of this.

"Truth or dare, Scarlett," he whispered, grazing the tips of his fingers across the back of her neck. She shivered.

"Dare," she said. He froze, and she turned her head in his direction. "I surprised you with that, didn't I? I want something good, Brody. Something hot. Something you want me to do."

His cock rose to half-mast as his mouth went dry. If this was her way of letting him know she was ready for a little more pushing, he was more than happy to oblige.

· · ·

Breath held, Scarlett waited for Brody's dare. She might have bitten off more than she could chew by being so brazen with her request, but the nerves that had been twisting her stomach, the doubt that was starting to creep in, were really pissing her off. She'd seen that she could get completely lost in the act of sex—things came out of her mouth when she was blinded by her body's desires.

That was huge. But she wanted to feel confident in *her* actions, not second-guess every word, every movement. She wanted to blind Brody with desire too.

And the only way she could do that was by taking the bull

by the horns and embracing the fact that she was capable of being sensual. It was time to get past the awkward.

"I dare you to dance for me."

Her lungs squeezed tight. Out of everything Brody could have requested, it never crossed her mind it would involve her most humiliating moment. She could still see her ex clutching his stomach as he doubled over with laughter on the couch. The saddest part was how she'd felt so sexy before his reaction. She had felt sexy the entire time she'd taken that class.

How *she* had felt was what she needed to embrace, not how Ryan had made her feel.

"Can you give me a few minutes?"

"Sure."

Grabbing her phone, Scarlett hurried into the bathroom, Princess trotting in after her. First, she had to prepare herself. Not that she had much with her. Just her phone case. As she placed her cell on the counter, she glanced in the long mirror over the dual sinks. Her hair needed some work after being smashed by the helmet, but her makeup was still on its A-game. Now for her outfit. Jeans and a halter top would not do.

"You can do this," she said to her reflection, as the cat jumped up on the counter and pushed her head into Scarlett's forearm.

She ran her hand down the feline's spine, her heart aching. This had been a night of facing a lot of insecurities created from the past. The cat, Brody's question about it, had been another moment where she'd been briefly swept back to a different time, a harder time. She'd given a piss poor excuse for never getting a cat; Brody had to know Ryan wasn't allergic. But the excuse had just popped out of her mouth because she couldn't voice the truth.

After it was clear Ryan would not proceed with any more treatment, she'd mentioned getting a cat. He'd accused her of wanting to replace a baby with an animal. If they couldn't have a baby, then they sure as hell weren't getting a cat. In hindsight, it was just another way for Ryan to punish her—he couldn't have what he wanted, so she wasn't going to get what she wanted.

She shook herself. No more past tonight. It had interfered more than she liked. All she needed to focus on right now was Brody and what was going to happen next.

It was time for her to take control of her sensuality.

Before she chickened out, she slipped off her heels then shed her jeans and halter top. The black, crochet lace, cheeky panty and matching push-up bra were more revealing than what she would've worn to perform this routine, but she was going for sexy and this was definitely sexy.

After she fluffed her hair, she picked up her phone, scrolled through her playlist, stopping on Christina Aguilera's song "Express" from the movie *Burlesque*. She turned down the volume so she could get the tune exactly where she wanted it to start. Once she was happy with it, she paused the song and turned the volume on max.

As she opened the bathroom door, she yelled, "Close your eyes and don't look until I say so."

"Yes, ma'am."

She stepped into the living to find Brody had taken a throw blanket and pressed it to his face. Smiling, she hurried into the dining area, grabbed one of the chairs, then positioned it in the middle of the living room with the back of the chair toward Brody.

She climbed up on top of the seat, balanced herself on one foot then crossed her other leg over the other one. She pressed play and dropped her phone on the floor. The sound of snapping fingers filled the room, and she quickly got into the rhythm before saying, "You can look."

The huge smile on Brody's face as he removed the

throw immediately turned to slack-jawed awe. He pushed up straighter, muttering, "Holy fuck."

She shifted her position then lowered her crossed leg to the ground, keeping the other bent up on the chair. There was no amusement, just blatant lust in his gaze. The heat made her nipples pucker into tight peaks as she moved off the chair then bent from the waist so her hands were around her ankles.

He growled from behind her, and it was an enthralling sound, giving her the strength, the courage, to proceed with the routine. Not once did he take his eyes off her. Not when she straddled the chair, not when she sensually swayed her hips, shook her breasts, or ran her hands over her body.

He was her captivated private audience, and she had never felt more beautiful than she did in those two minutes.

When the song wound down, she sashayed over to stand in front of him. "Truth or dare, Brody?"

"Dare." There was no denying the hunger deepening his voice.

"I dare you to make me come."

As the words passed her lips, a weight lifted from somewhere deep inside her. Over the years, she'd lost her faith in her sexual appeal. Brody had given it back by making her feel true lust for the first time.

He pulled her forward by the hips.

"Nothing would make me happier," he said, then tugged her onto his lap. His erection pressed into her ass as he leaned her back into his arms and took her lips in a deep kiss. His fingers slipped beneath the hem of her panties and found her aching clit. Turned on from the dance and his undivided, heated attention, it only took him seconds to get her off.

She moaned through the pleasure that sent pulsating waves through her. As she slowly drifted back, she lightly pushed Brody against the cushion, then repositioned so she straddled his hips.

Reaching down, she grabbed the hem of his shirt and tugged it over his head. Defined muscles greeted her—shoulder muscles, pecs, six-pack. They all beckoned, and she could touch anything she wanted.

Placing kisses along his chest, she moved her way down his rock-hard stomach until she knelt between his knees. There was only one place she was concentrating on. One more hurdle she needed to jump. Something she had not done in a long time because she'd felt so inept.

She popped the top button of Brody's jeans then carefully lowered the zipper over the huge bulge. He lifted his hips so she could tug his boxer briefs and pants down. Bottom lip tucked between her teeth, she inspected the huge, impressive…

Cock, Scarlett. It's okay to think it…to say it.

The reminder helped, but nerves hit her stomach, threatening to ruin her progress. She would not allow it. Never again. She could and would give a hell of a blow job.

Gently, she wrapped her fingers around him. Brody let out a harsh breath and shifted, but his gaze never strayed from her. He didn't lean his head back. Didn't close his eyes and just enjoy. He watched. Intently.

Desire flared through her. Apparently, she liked being watched. Leaning forward, she slowly slid him into her mouth, mindful to use her other hand to cup his balls. An approving grunt came out of him, and she looked up as she bobbed her head in slow, measured movements.

"Goddamn, that's a fucking gorgeous picture," he gritted out. As she continued, his lips suddenly pressed tight. "That's enough."

He grabbed her under the arms and hauled her up.

"But—"

"Any more and we're not going to finish this."

Then, he stood, snatched her around the waist, and flipped

her over so she was on her knees on the cushions. Positioned behind her, he walked forward, forcing her to move to the end of the couch until her thighs met the arm. "Stay right there," he said.

Glancing over her shoulder, she watched him kick off his shoes and shuck his pants off the rest of the way. He reached into the jeans, grabbed his wallet, and withdrew a condom. Quickly, he slid it on and was right back behind her. The warmth of his palm rubbed her ass before he tugged her panties down.

"What do you want, Scarlett?" he asked.

"You," she said instantly.

"Me to do what?"

Her entire body screamed to have him inside her. "Fuck me. Hard."

Then he was, stretching her, filling her, and it felt amazing.

"Spread your legs wider."

She did as he instructed.

"Now rub your clit for me, Scarlett," he said breathlessly between deep, fast thrusts. "I want to watch you come again."

She slipped her arm underneath her body. A sharp smack stung her ass cheek and sent shards of pleasure racing through her as his other hand gripped her hip. A moan ripped out of her mouth. "Come for me, baby."

The sound of their skin slapping together, the crack of his hand occasionally meeting her butt, the sweet pain that felt so good… Her orgasm hit her hard, and she groaned. Brody stiffened behind her with a long, blissful grunt.

Scarlett collapsed over the armrest, trying to get her breath. Never in her life had she experienced something like that. Now knew what she had been missing out on all these years.

Sex could be amazing. As long as it was with the right person.

Chapter Eight

Scarlett's phone dinged and giddiness immediately had her reaching across the bed to grab the device.

For the past week, Brody had sent her a text at nine on the dot every night. It was crazy how much she looked forward to hearing from him. There was never anything intimate — mostly just a friendly check-in, how was her day type text. She never texted him first, though. She wanted to, but it was one of those things she hesitated on because she wasn't sure if her contacting him was appropriate, especially since his messages were so short and sweet.

Do you have plans tomorrow night?

A grin sprang to her lips. He wanted to see her.

She wanted to see him. Badly. She hadn't really been prepared for how their night out would end, which had been with him driving her home in the wee morning hours after they'd had another amazing round of sex. He'd walked her to the door like a gentleman, but he hadn't kissed her or even mentioned getting together again soon. Nor had he all week.

Unfortunately, that had caused some of the insecurity she'd thought she'd dealt with to come roaring back. More than once this week, she'd worried that maybe Brody hadn't had as much fun as she had. She'd pushed her doubts aside, reminding herself that this was what Brody referred to as an "adult relationship." They weren't dating.

But it was hard to understand the rules, which was why she was grateful he at least texted each day.

Not at the moment, she typed.

A few moments later, her phone dinged again.

Good. You're mine then.

A little thrill went through her. She didn't know what it was about the possessive undertones of the text that pleased her so much, but being called *his* definitely made her happy.

A tap sounded on her door.

"Yeah?"

Delaney poked her head in. "I see from the smile, you got your nightly text."

"And we're getting together tomorrow night."

"Oo la la. Going to get some more of that good Brody lovin'?"

Scarlett laughed. "Definitely."

Delaney stepped inside the room then came to sit on the edge of the bed. "It's good to see you smiling, Scar."

She guessed she had been doing a lot of that this week. She'd even caught herself humming the other day.

"It's good to feel light."

After dealing with such heavy, depressing emotions for so long, she'd forgotten what it was like to just *be*. For the first time in a long time, that was exactly what she was doing. No worries about things she couldn't control. No constant thoughts revolving around about her ugly past. Merely enjoying the anticipation of hearing from Brody, even if it was only a couple of texts a night.

Silence fell between them, then Scarlett asked, "Can I ask you something?"

"Anything, babe."

"With the type of arrangement I have with Brody, should I be this excited to see or hear from him?"

Delaney crossed her arms and studied her thoughtfully. "Do you want my honest opinion?"

"Always."

"I've never done a casual setup with a friend, Scar. It seems like it could get sticky pretty quickly."

That's what she was worried about.

"What do I need to do to keep things casual? It gets so confusing. No holding hands. No spending the night. Enjoy yourself. Don't read too much into it—"

"Okay, I get it." Delaney held up her hand, chuckling. "Look the only thing you can do is be honest with yourself. Some people aren't cut out for casual. If the arrangement is no longer working for you…" Delaney trailed off, shrugging.

It wasn't so much the situation didn't work. Her conflicting thoughts were what confused her. A no-strings-attached agreement with a man she found insanely attractive was what she wanted. So why did it feel like something was missing?

• • •

"Great session," Brody said, pulling off his protective headgear.

"You're looking real good. Keep it up," his sparring partner Matt said.

He'd been training with Mike and his crew for a little over a week now. It was amazing how differently he was treated here. Mike didn't play favorites. If he was working with someone one-on-one, that person got his full attention. If the fighters were working with his crew, Mike would walk around overseeing each session with the co-trainers, stepping in when he needed to.

The man was brimming with superior knowledge. Brody had already learned a few new techniques.

He climbed out of the ring as Mike stepped out of his office.

"Brody!" When he glanced in his coach's direction, Mike signaled for Brody to come over, and he made his way across the gym to stand in the doorway. Mike was back behind his desk.

"Close the door and have a seat."

Short and blunt. Typical Mike, he was learning, but his stomach knotted for an instant. Had he done something wrong?

He was trying to prove himself to this man. So far, he hadn't gotten anything from Mike on how bad or how good he was. All the man did was focus on weaknesses, and what to do to fix it.

He sat in the worn leather chair, bracing his elbows on his knees. "What's up?"

Mike leaned back in his chair and crossed his arms behind his head. There was a clear sense of triumph oozing off the man. "I just got off the phone with Ethan."

There was only one Ethan he could be talking about. Ethan Porter—the president of CMC.

Brody sat up a little straighter. "Yeah? For?"

"Jack Raster was injured in practice yesterday. He's bowing out of your fight to recoup."

It felt like he'd just received a huge blow to the gut. He wasn't sure why Mike looked so goddamn pleased, either. Yeah, Brody wasn't happy about who he'd been matched up with for his next appearance in the cage, but losing a fight completely sucked.

"What does that mean?" Brody asked.

"You ready to really prove yourself? Shut-up some naysayers?"

Unease shimmied through him. "How?"

"I've been in negotiation all morning with Ethan and Greg."

At the mention of his former trainer, he stiffened. "Greg?"

Mike leaned forward. "Seems the moment Greg heard about Raster's injury, he went to Ethan with a proposition. He wants you to put your money—or your fighting skills, as the case may be—where your mouth is. You against Randy Boss."

A whirring sound entered his head as he digested the information. Fuck, he'd really pissed Greg off. The man was making a serious point. Brody either had to show up or shut up. Now he was getting the chance to beat the much talked about and highly anticipated up-and-comer, and it could either royally fuck his career or revive it.

"Brody?"

He started then swallowed. "That's awesome."

"There's a stipulation, though, made by Greg."

That wasn't surprising. "And it is?"

"The fight has to be in two weeks."

Brody pressed his lips together as he slowly nodded, taking in what Mike was telling him. With only two weeks to train, Brody wouldn't be as prepared as he would have been if it was scheduled for the original date. He didn't doubt for one minute that Greg was going to work the headlines on this matchup, either, making the pressure on him even worse. But this was his chance to shine.

"Sign it," he instructed.

He just hoped he didn't fall flat on his face.

• • •

Scarlett studied Brody across the table. Ever since he'd picked her up an hour ago to take her for a late lunch, he'd seemed distant. Trying to have a conversation with him had been like pulling teeth. "Everything okay?"

He glanced up from cutting into his chicken Marsala. "What?"

And that was the way things had been going all afternoon.

In body, he was here, but his mind was not—something she had dealt a lot with over the last few years. Inattention. Distraction. Feeling like she was alone even with her companion in the same room. It wasn't fair to Brody, but she couldn't stop the tightening in her chest or the thoughts that started bombarding her. Was he already growing bored with her? Though things had gone beyond great—at least for her—maybe they hadn't for him.

He had texted her during the week, kept in contact, she reminded herself. On the other hand, he hadn't called or tried to set up anything during the week. But that was their agreement. It was supposed to be casual. Yet, he wasn't interacting with her now. Seemed like if he wanted to spend time with her in the same way she couldn't wait to spend time with him, then he would be more involved than he was right now.

God, her mind was driving her insane.

"If you just want to call it a night after dinner, we can." The words just spewed out of her mouth, driven by the thoughts that refused to shut up.

He blinked at her. "Why would I want to do that?"

The very blunt answer eased some of her tension. At least he hadn't jumped at the out she was giving him. "I don't know. You seem distracted tonight."

He laid his fork down beside his plate. "I *am* distracted tonight, and I apologize for that. You should be getting my full attention."

The fact that he owned up to it immediately, and didn't try to convince her she was being oversensitive, surprised her. She wasn't used to a man owing up to his failures or apologizing for it. All it made her want to do was help in some way. "Something bothering you?"

"Nah. Just thinking about my game plan, and I shouldn't be bringing work in our time together."

So he was upset over work. She hated the relief she felt; she didn't want anything to be bugging him, but at least it wasn't her. "Did something happen today?"

"My opponent got hurt, and I was scheduled for a new fight."

This had happened before, back when Brody was around a lot. An unexpected fight change was a lot of hard work for him, since he would have been training to go up against a specific person. "Is he a totally different fighter than who you'd been matched with?"

He inhaled. "Yeah. Big time. It's a big fight for me. I have to win it."

Brody had never worried about an opponent he was going up against. At least, not that she knew of. "Why is this one so important?"

"Because I ran off at the mouth, pissed off Greg, and now I have to prove myself."

"Greg? Your coach?"

"Ex-coach."

When had Brody left Greg's? It bothered her that he hadn't shared that with her. *But you're not dating, girl.* Conversations about his day at work weren't her privilege. Why did she hate that? "Who are you training with?"

"Mike."

"What happened with Greg?"

"Long story, but the gist is he sided with the articles that came out after my last fight."

"What articles?"

A patient smile graced his lips. "The ones saying I was at the end of my career."

She gasped in outrage. "You're not at the end of your career!"

"As much as I love the vote of confidence, Scarlett, the articles had a point. I haven't been advancing for the last couple of years. I've been stagnating."

She didn't like the defeated way Brody sounded right now. It reminded her a lot of where she'd been before she'd left Ryan. One amazing night with Brody and he'd helped her extinguish some of her self-doubt. Not all, but it was a step in the right direction. Now it was her turn to boost his self-confidence.

"Do you know what I see when I look at you, Brody Minton?"

"What?"

"A man who doesn't give up, who stands up for what he believes in, and never settles for anything less than what he deserves. I have no doubt that you'll go into that cage and show everyone that a couple of flawed fights mean nothing. You're still a damn great cage fighter." She reached across the table and squeezed his hand. "Don't let the haters get into your head. Once you do, it's hard to get them out. Trust me, I know. You have to believe in yourself. No one else's opinion matters."

But his gaze had dropped from hers and was latched on their hands. She hadn't even thought about the gesture, she'd just done it. Had she crossed some line? Clearing her throat, she slowly slid her hand off his and back to her side of the table. She hated this. She didn't know how to do an adult relationship. She knew it meant no intimacy—handholding, kissing, etc.—but she questioned everything she did outside the bedroom. At least in there, she seemed to be doing a pretty good job.

"Thank you, Scarlett. I needed to hear that. Because you're right. I let the opinions of others get to me."

"If it's any consolation, I believe in you. Always have. Always will."

Their gazes connected, and Brody's Adam's apple bobbed. "You're an amazing woman. Any man is going to be damn lucky to have you standing in his corner."

"I'm standing in yours."

Brody shook his head, blowing out a harsh breath, breaking the intimate moment they'd just shared. And there was no other word for what had just transpired between them. She'd spoken to him like a partner would. Building him up. Supporting him. And it felt right. Natural.

"How are things going your way?" he asked as he picked his up fork and continued eating, as if nothing weird just happened.

How did Brody feel about the unexpected intimacy? Other than flat out asking him and making things awkward, she wouldn't know. Right now, she was okay with that. She needed to figure out what it meant to her, first.

"Enjoying summer break. It's giving me time to get my life organized before school starts back. I'm going to stay with Delaney for a while *and*…I filed for divorce. Once Ryan signs it, too, it'll be finalized within thirty-one days."

He didn't respond, just chewed his food, a far-away look to his eyes. Was he lost in his fight again?

"And you'll officially be a single woman." He stabbed a piece a chicken a little too hard with his fork and then shoved it into his mouth.

No. It wasn't the fight bothering him this time. She got the distinct impression that he didn't like the idea of her being single, which didn't make any sense.

Instead of dwelling on it, she changed the subject again.

"So, what're we doing today?"

Whatever had been going on in his mind vanished as he sent her a smile and a wink. "It's a big surprise."

A surprise. So, even though he wasn't really talking to her during the week, he was arranging surprises for her. A giddy, happy feeling warmed her chest.

• • •

"Oh my God!" Scarlett all but squealed. "It's Deadpool. Take a picture, Brody!"

The grin on his face hurt as she raced from his side and all but tackled the man dressed up as her all-time favorite superhero. The woman had not stopped posing with the cosplayers since she'd walked into the convention. Rick Grimes, Iron Man, and Thor were only a few she'd stopped to take a photo with.

He snapped a picture of the two of them, then Scarlett returned to his side, full of bouncing energy. His plan was working. The last time they'd gone out, he'd focused on the sex part. Today was about having fun together and showing her there was more between them than just an attraction.

One way to make sure that happened was to bring in the love they both had for geek shit. His was comic books. Hers were superhero movies, *The Walking Dead*, *Doctor Who*, and an assortment of other shows.

"This is so awesome! I've always wanted to come to one of these conventions."

He was glad he was the man who'd brought her to her first con. Hopefully it wouldn't be the last. This one was small. The big one, Dragon*Con, was in a few months. She'd shit herself over that event.

Brody glanced at the time on his phone. They had just a few minutes to get to her big surprise. She was going to fucking flip. He pulled the ticket he'd spent seventy dollars on out of the back pocket of his jeans.

"We need to go in there." He pointed to a large ballroom filled with people waiting in long lines for photo ops with their favorite stars. As he handed the ticket to the attendee, who pointed them to the correct line, Scarlett's eyes got huge.

"Are you serious?" she whispered. "Norman Reedus?" She spun on him, a manic look in her eyes. "I'm going to *touch* Norman Reedus?"

He didn't know about all that, now. "I paid for a picture, Scarlett. Not for you to maul him."

She cupped her hands to her mouth, her body vibrating with her excitement. He grinned again. He loved making her this happy.

Then she exploded toward him, launching into his arms, and smashed her mouth to his, repeating, "Thank you," against his lips. The kiss was so unexpected, he stiffened for a second before he tugged her closer. Instantly, she melted against his chest, then her body went rigid and she jerked back.

Staring up at him, she grimaced and twisted her fingers together in obvious agitation. "I'm sorry. That was inappropriate."

Those goddamn boundaries again. He hated the limitations of their arrangement.

"Don't ever apologize for kissing me, Scarlett."

Biting her bottom lip, she nodded then turned to face the front of the line. Tension radiated from her body.

He'd succeeded in one thing. She hadn't just thanked him with a quick hug, like she used to do. No, she'd thrown herself at him and kissed him.

That was a move in the right direction. But the weirdness between them concerned him. Things had been going great. Now, he had to bring the fun back.

Fifteen minutes later, she was bouncing beside him again.

Wearing a dark pair of sunglasses, Norman Reedus stood right in front of them, taking a picture with another fan.

"Oh my God," she repeated. "I'm next. Oh my God."

He grinned. Yeah, things had gotten a little tense, but he would go through that awkwardness all over again to see her like this.

The fan walked off, and Scarlett bolted forward, starry eyes on her favorite TV hero. She went to stand beside him, and Reedus slipped his arm around her shoulder…and she giggled. That giggle got an outright laugh from him. She was so giddy she could barely contain herself.

The moment was over fast. The picture was taken, Reedus said something to her, and Scarlett started walking toward Brody, dazed.

As she reached his side, she mumbled, "Norman Reedus touched me."

Again, he laughed, and not giving damn about what their relationship was or was not, he tugged her to his side as he steered them out of the conference room.

She tilted her head up toward him. "You're totally getting fucked tonight."

His mouth went dry. "Promise?"

"Oh, yeah. I'm jumping your ass as soon as we get back to my place."

Then she pulled away, putting distance between them. He wanted to tug her back, but she was making a lot clear. Apologizing for the kiss, making sure they kept the appropriate distance when they hung out, pulling her hand away from his over dinner—she wanted to keep things like they had agreed upon.

"Your place? What about Delaney?" he asked, trying to focus on something other than what *he* wanted.

"She's out for the night with a few friends. There's some kind of music event going on at Centennial Olympic Park."

She laughed softly. "Music and that park. She's in hog heaven right now."

"The music I get, but the park throws me some. Why is she in hog heaven at the park?" he asked.

"It's one of her favorite places to relax and take what she calls her down-time pictures. At least three times a week, she eats her lunch out there and snaps photos for her portfolio."

"That's cool."

"I don't think anything is going to top meeting Norman Reedus. You ready to get out of here?"

A grin sprang to his lips. "Oh, yeah. I'm more than ready."

• • •

The moment Scarlett opened the door to her place, she spun around grabbed Brody by the T-shirt and yanked him inside. Throwing her arms around his neck, she latched her mouth onto his. As his tongue sailed past her lips, and he walked her backward toward the couch, she groaned.

Maybe she was being a little too eager, but with them like this, tugging off each other's shirts, kissing as if they'd never kiss again, there was no questioning herself. No hesitation. No doubt.

And she'd wanted to kiss—really kiss—Brody all afternoon. She was mentally exhausted from fighting the impulse.

She ripped her mouth away from his and fumbled with the button of his jeans, feeling rejuvenated. She was ready to have him. Right here in the living room. And he seemed just as impatient as he worked on her shorts.

As her button released, she pushed them and her panties over her hips and let them fall to the floor. A deep rattle of approval vibrated out of Brody as he grabbed the condom out of his wallet then did the same with his jeans and boxer briefs.

One quick flick to the back of her bra, and they stood in her living room naked, panting and sexually charged.

Her eyes roamed over him, feasting on the gorgeous display of muscles and the proud cock that made him all man. Desire heated her insides as she dropped to her knees before him, took him into her hand, and lowered her head.

She wanted a taste. A small, quick taste. It was something new that Brody brought to life inside her.

Blow jobs before had been a chore. She hadn't enjoyed giving them, but did them anyway, because it was part of sex. With Brody, she wanted him in her mouth, wanted to hear the grunts she brought out of him with her slow suction. And he cooperated. With each bob, his breathing became choppy, his hips jutted forward to greet her open mouth, his hand tangled in the hair at her nape.

"Fuck," he muttered as his grip tightened on the strands, giving that splendid sharp tug she enjoyed so much. She moaned around him.

Fuck was right. She liked fucking this man. Any way. Anywhere. She finally felt empowered as a sexual being. She had him in the palm of her hand—literally and figuratively.

All because she had finally embraced herself. Believed in herself and her abilities inside the bedroom.

Brody had given that back to her.

"Stop," he muttered as he pulled his hips backward, away from her mouth.

No questions as to why sprang into her mind. No worries she was doing it wrong taunted her. All she felt was complete womanly satisfaction at bringing him that close to coming, and a wicked grin stretched her lips.

"Woman," he said, with a raw husky edge. "You and that mouth. Damn."

Her grin only spread. Brody tugged her up then lifted her into his arms. She let out a surprised little yelp. "What're you doing?"

"My mouth has a craving right now, too."

He carried her over to the couch, gently sat her down, then lowered to his knees in front of her. Without hesitation, she parted her legs.

"I love seeing you like this."

She loved being like this. As he lowered his head, she thread her fingers through his hair and gave herself over to the splendid sensations that his mouth evoked through her body. She allowed herself to be selfish. Allowed it to be only about her. Didn't worry about time, or how long he was down there, or why she wasn't coming. She simply *was*.

And she couldn't think of another place she'd rather be than with Brody creating these sensations over and over again.

Hours passed in sex-filled haze on the couch, in the kitchen, and finally in her bed. They took turns teasing, kissing, fucking…coming, until she felt like there wasn't a muscle left in her body.

Everything about this night had been wonderful. She shifted to her side to face Brody, who was lying on his back with one arm raised above his head on the pillow, a weird expression on his face. Definitely not like the relaxed one he'd had from the moment she'd dropped to her knees in front of him.

"You all right?" she asked.

He jerked a little and then turned his head toward her with a strained smile. "Fuck, yeah, I'm great. You know how to suck the energy right out of a man." He fell silent for a second before saying, "I need to get home."

A heavy feeling settled in her stomach. She didn't want him to go. She wanted him to stay right here with her. Wanted to know that she'd see him again tomorrow. That it wouldn't be another week before they went out again.

Everything about this was confusing. She didn't want a relationship, but at the same time, that was exactly what she wanted—with Brody.

As he heaved himself out of the bed in all his naked glory, her eyes hungrily raked over the defined muscles, not knowing when she'd see him like this again. He walked toward the hall where his clothes were laying and said, "I'll text you."

Then he was gone. No kiss. No good-bye. Nothing.

And she hated it.

Chapter Nine

Brody weaved around Blake's jab then countered with a left hook into his side. Blake dropped his hands then bounced back as he ripped the headgear off.

"You're looking good there, cuz." Blake slipped between the second and third rope and jumped to the floor.

Pulling off his own headgear, Brody followed his cousin out of the ring to a bench. Blake handed him a cold water bottle. "Thanks."

He sat down beside Blake, and they both drank their water in silence for a few moments before Blake asked, "What're you plans tonight?"

"Taking Scarlett out."

It'd been another long fucking week of not seeing her and trying to keep things casual.

He could feel his cousin's gaze on the side of his face, but he avoided making eye contact, worried he'd read more in his expression than Brody wanted him to see.

"How's that working for you?"

Like shit. "Good."

"Yeah, I believe that. My guess is the reason you keep checking your phone after each session is you're looking to see if she texted. You can't get her out of your head, can you?"

He never should've told the ass anything. Brody glared at him for being a goddamn know-it-all.

But Blake was right. He did keep checking his phone to see if she'd contacted him. Why he was driving himself crazy with that was beyond him. She had never initiated texting him. Seemed she had a much easier time during their days apart than he did, and it bugged the shit out of him.

Because he hated texting. He only allowed himself to do it because he had to reach out to her somehow. What he really wanted to do was call just to hear her voice, talk about their day, laugh together. Though Scarlett probably wouldn't think twice about him doing so, for him, personally, he would be crossing a line. He couldn't treat her like a girlfriend. He either had to be her friend, which he didn't think he could go back to, or a woman he only had sex with—which was no longer working for him, either, because he wanted to do stupid couple shit with her.

He didn't know what to do.

"Yeah. You can't." Blake answered his own question, then gave a disgusted scoff and shook his head. "I knew this was a bad idea the moment you told me about it. You can't go into an arrangement like that with a woman you're already feeling for. You're setting yourself up for failure, bro."

No-fucking-duh. "I couldn't let her do this with another man, either."

"Man, you've got yourself fucked into a corner. What are you going to do about it?"

That's the question he'd been asking himself since he'd left her bed and forced himself to walk out of her house in the early morning hours—almost a week ago, now. He was being very careful to space their "dates" out. Lot of good it was doing, though. She drove him crazy when they weren't together and then drove him crazy when they were.

Fucking ridiculous.

"I've got to win her."

Blake clapped him hard on the back. "There you go. Go after what you want. It's a shit-ton better than this limbo you're in with her."

Brody took a long drag off the water bottle. Again, Blake was right. They'd only made the arrangement a little over two weeks ago, but he was quickly learning he couldn't keep sex separated from emotion—at least, not where Scarlett was concerned. He didn't want to spook her, either. A slow build would be the best approach. Holding her hand, kissing outside of foreplay and sex. Real couple shit.

Tonight, he'd experiment with it.

"Umm," Blake hedged. "Scarlett is living with Delaney, right?"

Brody studied his cousin. Blake had brought up Delaney more than once, and at weird times. "Dude, are you interested in her or something?"

"Nah. At least, not in the way you're thinking." He sighed. "We hooked up in the Bahamas, and, you know… I live here. She lives here. I wouldn't mind revisiting that."

"I can ask Scarlett for Delaney's number."

"What are we, fifteen? No numbers. *But*, maybe probe around and see if you can figure out where she likes to hang at. I'll arrange an accidental bump-into."

"I can help with that. Scarlett mentioned Delaney likes to eat her lunch at Centennial a few times a week to take pictures."

"Just a few times a week? No actual routine."

"I didn't ask. She just mentioned it."

"Well, that's better than nothing." Blake clapped him on the shoulder again. "Thanks, cuz. Now I need to get showered.

I'm taking Mom to dinner tonight. It's her birthday, and she's been real down in the dumps this week, missing Dad."

"Have fun."

He watched Blake hurry into the locker room. Ever since his father had died, he'd been trying to keep his mom busy. But after losing her husband of thirty years, Aunt Bell just wasn't the same anymore. He'd give Blake props for trying, though. He tried to make his mom smile whenever he could.

Brody stood and headed for the locker room, too. He had no plans to shower here. He had to go home and get ready for a serious night of courting.

Operation "Win Scarlett's heart" would officially start.

• • •

Something felt different about tonight.

Scarlett smiled her thanks to Brody as she slipped her hand into the crook of his offered elbow. He led her from the fancy Italian restaurant and out onto the downtown Atlanta sidewalk.

Three hours ago, she'd received a text from him that said, *Dress up.*

So she'd put on the dress that she'd bought for their first night out. Brody had shown up looking handsome and sexy in black slacks and a silky, button-down, bright blue shirt.

Dinner had a very romantic feel to it. Brody had sat across from her, his face shadowed from the dim lights inside the restaurant. A single flicking flame from the candle in the middle of the table gave them most of their light. Classical music played in the background. Everything was hushed. Softened.

If she didn't know better, she'd believe that she and Brody were on an official date. But that couldn't be the case. Maybe he was just in the mood for something a little different tonight. There was nothing wrong with wanting to get dressed up and go out—even if it was with someone you were only supposed to be having sex with.

Her feelings after Brody had left that night had led to a week of internal debate about what she wanted. In the end, she had to take the advice Delaney had given her. She had to be honest with herself. Once she stopped letting her brain convince her that she wasn't ready for a relationship, and allowed her heart to take the lead, everything fell into place.

She wasn't the kind of girl who could do a casual, friends-with-benefits deal. She wasn't made that way—she sure as hell wasn't made to have amazing sex then be dropped off at her apartment or left behind afterward. She missed him too much during the week and was way too excited when he finally reached out to her.

She *wanted* a relationship with Brody instead of this casual affair. He was open to that, he'd said as much when he'd come to her the first time. Now it was her turn to come to him.

She tilted her head to give him a side glance as they strolled through downtown Atlanta. "Dinner was amazing. Thank you."

He gave her a pleased smile. "I'm glad you liked it."

She slid her hand from his elbow and down his forearm, then linked their fingers together. Brody's eyes shot down to their joined hands, then back up to hers. Questions resided there.

"What do you have planned next, Mr. Minton?"

"I thought we'd take a carriage ride."

"I like that. Will you put your arm around me?"

He stopped walking and pivoted his body toward her. She could feel his intense gaze all the way to her core. "I'd love nothing more," he whispered.

She caught her bottom lip between her teeth to cover the

thrilled smile. Because she'd love nothing more, too.

Brody led her down the sidewalk then stopped in front of one the carriages and paid the driver. After they were seated, he wrapped his arm around her and tucked her close to his side. He threaded the fingers of his other hand with hers. Her heart squeezed tight.

Being in Brody's arms like this felt so right.

They rode in silence. She paid no attention to the passing scenery. None of it mattered. What did was being here with Brody, the feel of his lips skimming across her forehead, his fingers tightening around hers, the weight of his arm pressing her into his side.

She felt loved and cherished, and it was amazing—even more powerful than being sexually awakened.

Was it possible that she and Brody were meant to be?

Everything about them was compatible. After falling in love once and seeing how badly her marriage had ended, the idea of allowing someone that close again was terrifying. But Brody was getting under her skin. She had two options: end things with him, or allow them to progress to a real relationship.

She had promised herself she was putting her happiness first.

Brody made her happy.

And he was worth taking another stab at this love thing.

• • •

He'd held Scarlett in his arms like a true partner.

That thought kept revolving in his head as they drove back to his place. Something had changed between them. Something big. He hadn't wanted to ask during the carriage ride, not while finally holding her the way he'd craved for years, but now it was time to see if they were on the same page. The last thing he wanted was to scare her off because of his hopeful thinking.

He glanced over at her, sitting in the passenger seat of his car, staring out the window. Her features were relaxed, as if nothing were on her mind. That was good. Scarlett wore her emotions on her sleeve.

"Scarlett?"

"Hmm?"

"Am I taking you home tonight?" It was the only question that he had to ask, as far as he was concerned. That answer would give him all the information he needed on how to proceed.

She turned her head toward him, and the sweetest smile graced her lips as she looked at him. "No."

His chest expanded with shock and excitement. It had happened. After all these years, Scarlett was his. *His.*

An answering grin pulled at his mouth. "Okay."

He pressed the gas pedal closer to the floor.

Ten minutes later, he pulled into the garage. Nervous energy coursed through him, making his palms sweat. Tonight he wouldn't just fuck Scarlett—they'd make love.

After they rode up in the elevator to his condo, they stepped inside. The last time they'd gone out, they hadn't made it past the threshold before Scarlett was on him. He didn't want it to be like that tonight. He wanted to enjoy not only her body, but being with her.

As Scarlett turned toward him, her intent evident on her face, he immediately stopped it with, "Want to watch a movie?"

Surprise crossed her features as she digested his words. "That sounds fun."

Curling up on the couch with the woman he'd loved secretly from afar, now knowing he could love on her openly, any fucking time he wanted, did sound fun.

"Go get on the couch. I'll get everything ready."

After she sat down, Princess already climbing onto her lap, he picked a comedy from his collection, popped it into the DVD player, then turned off all the lights so the glow from the television was the only light in the room. When he turned back to find Scarlett whispering to his cat as she stroked its fur, his breath caught tight in his lungs, causing an ache in his chest.

Scarlett was his. She was in his home, on his couch, petting his cat. Though she'd stated otherwise just a few weeks ago, she didn't want a no-strings-attached arrangement any longer. She wanted strings. She wanted attachment. With him.

She'd chosen to be with him all on her own.

Euphoria hit him. He no longer had to keep his distance. No longer had to control his emotions for this woman. They were finally going to get their chance at happiness. A possible future together.

Something he never believed he'd get a chance to have with her.

She looked up, and her eyes rounded. "What?"

"Just taking in how beautiful you are, and how lucky I am."

Pleasure brightened her face as she patted the cushion beside her. "Cuddle with me."

He didn't have to be asked twice. He rushed to take the seat next to her. Scarlett sat up and gently lowered Princess to the floor, then she repositioned herself so she was curled into his side, cheek pressed against his chest, hand resting on his stomach. Brody lowered his arm around her shoulders.

Emotions clogged his throat, and he swallowed hard. Fucking Scarlett had been an unforgettable moment. But holding her intimately meant so much more to him. He kissed the top of her head.

She tilted her head back to look at him, their lips only

inches apart. As they stared at each other, the air grew heavy around them. He'd kissed her, yes, but they'd always been lust induced. Though his hunger for this woman would never abate, he wanted to truly kiss her for the first time. Slow. Thorough.

He brushed his mouth across hers, then did it again. When her palm cupped his cheek, he deepened the kiss, tugging her closer to his side. As he swept his tongue inside, she strained up toward him. Using all his self-control, he ripped his mouth from hers and turned his attention back to the television.

"Brody?"

"Right now, I just want this."

He felt her gaze on him, but he kept his focus on the movie. Finally, she snuggled back against him, laid her head on his chest, and linked their fingers together.

A contented smile turned up his lips. Right now, just holding her was enough.

• • •

Tonight had been wonderful.

Scarlett tugged on the black T-shirt Brody had lent her to wear to bed. The hem stopped mid-thigh, and it was at least three sizes too big on her, but a warm rush of emotions washed over her. She'd loved the intimacy they'd shared so far tonight.

It'd been so long since she'd been held sweetly, like she meant the world to someone.

And now she was going to share his bed, not to just have fun, but to sleep. Such a small thing, really, but for them, it was a huge step in their relationship.

Did he snore? Was he a cover hog? Restless sleeper?

The questions popping into her head made her smile. Yeah, she'd been adamant that she didn't want anything serious with a man, but she didn't have any hesitation in her choice now. She looked forward to waking up to his handsome face in the morning. To starting a new routine with him.

She opened the bathroom door and stepped into his bedroom. Shirtless, Brody was lying on his side, head propped up on his palm, already on the left side of the king-sized mattress under the dark– and light-gray checkered comforter. Her heart squeezed tight.

"Goddamn, you're beautiful in my shirt."

This was really it. She was entering into a committed relationship, and nothing felt wrong about it. She walked over to her side of the bed then climbed under the silky, charcoal sheets. Pulling the cover up, she shifted onto her side and mimicked Brody's position, facing him.

He reached under the covers and ran his palm up and down her hip. It was a soothing action, and intimate one, and she loved it.

"Do you have any plans for tomorrow?" he asked.

"Nope."

"Would you like to go have dinner with my family?"

The invitation surprised her. He wanted her to meet his family?

"I know that seems a little rushed," he hurried to say, "but we always have dinner on Sunday. To be frank, I'm not ready to let you go back home yet. I want to spend tomorrow with you, too."

"I'd love to go."

"Good." He leaned in and kissed her. Closing her eyes, she enjoyed the sweet grazing of his mouth, the light nip on her bottom lip before he dragged her close to his chest and deepened the kiss. She wound one arm around his shoulder then rolled onto her back so he was above her.

There was nothing hurried about his kiss, no demanding need. It was slow, sensual, and just as hot as when he kissed her stupid. Her body buzzed to life. Her nipples hardened. It didn't matter how this man touched her, she responded, ached for him.

His hand slid down her side to the hem of her shirt. A second later he had it pulled over her head and tossed onto the floor. He lowered his head, taking her nipple into his mouth. Gasping, she threaded her fingers into his thick hair, arching toward him. He took his time, loving each breast with both his hands and mouth until she was whimpering and shifting on the bed.

He was torturing her with this restrained lovemaking. While it built a fire in her that was about to combust, she wanted, needed, him.

"Brody, please."

"What do you want, Scarlett?"

It was a question he'd asked her a few times while they'd been fucking. But tonight there was only one way she wanted to answer. "Make love to me."

Happiness lightened his light brown gaze. "Nothing would please me more."

Reaching onto the nightstand, he grabbed the condom he'd placed there. Within seconds, he had it ripped open and rolled on. He pushed himself up and over her then settled between her legs.

"This is how I've always wanted to be with you, Scarlett...a true couple."

Warmth spread across her chest, and she felt his words to her very core.

Then he took her lips in a searing kiss as he slowly thrust inside her. His loving, his touches, were all so gentle, so sweet, it brought a rush of emotions over her. Tears burned the back of her eyes.

She never believed she'd mean this much to someone again, but it was in everything he did. As they climaxed together, words she had no right to say yet pushed at the back of her throat, and she swallowed them.

Now wasn't the time to voice them. But one day, she would.

Because she couldn't imagine a life without Brody in it. Couldn't imagine anything tearing them apart.

Chapter Ten

Scarlett knew Brody had a huge family, but the reality of so many people was much more overwhelming than she'd expected. And not all of his sisters were even here—only three of them.

Savannah, the oldest sister, was hosting the family gathering with her husband and three daughters. Tessa was staying with Savannah, and the second to oldest, Maggie, was here with her husband and daughter. All the kids were under the age of five.

Chaos was the only way to describe what she was witnessing. The backyard was a madhouse. Bubbles, hula hoops, sidewalk chalk, screaming...

And the family gathered like this every Sunday... *Every Sunday*.

Strong hands latched onto her shoulders and kneaded. "About driven crazy yet?"

Smiling, she reached up and squeezed one of Brody's hands. At least he could acknowledge this was outside her comfort area. "There sure are a lot of you."

He chuckled behind her, giving her muscles another wonderful knead. "Yes, there are. It'll just get bigger, too. Tessa, Heather, Rikki, and I haven't gotten married or had kids yet."

At the mention of kids, her heart twisted. Not that she'd forgotten about her infertility. A person just didn't forget about that, but for the first time in years, Brody had her living in the moment. Since she'd been seeing him, she couldn't remember once thinking about not being able to have children.

It had been a much needed break. But the issue now roared back to the surface. Brody would want kids one day. How would he handle the news of her infertility?

It was a conversation she wasn't looking forward to, and one she wasn't ready to have yet. It was too early. They were just getting to know each other on a different level. Bringing up serious topics would only cause needless worry. The best thing to do was just enjoy each other right now.

"Uncle Brody! Come play with me!" his four-year old niece Ellie yelled, waving a hula hoop over her head—the fourth time, so far, she'd asked Brody to play with her.

"Duty calls." He leaned over and gave her a swift kiss on the lips then jogged over to his niece, grabbing her around the waist and spinning her in the air. A loud, childish squeal pierced the air, and Scarlett couldn't help a sad smile.

There was so much love in this family. It was in every square foot of the backyard, in the way the family laughed together and teased each other, in the happy children that ran around.

Before it'd all gone to crap, her family had been like that. One thing had changed it all. For her dad, it had been losing his job. For her mom, it'd been when he'd cheated. For Ryan, her infertility. For herself, Ryan getting another woman pregnant.

One moment, one decision, one life hurdle could be

the obstacle that destroyed the love between two people, breeding bitterness and resentment instead.

Brody's mother Elise came to stand beside her, an affectionate smile on her face as she watched her only son play with his niece. Not for the first time since she'd stepped into this house, Scarlett wondered how Brody's parents had beaten the odds.

"I love watching those two together," Elise said.

Brody was dramatically failing at hula hooping. He'd lift the hoop to his waist, rotate his hips, then let go of it. It would fall straight down to his feet. His theatrical groan made Ellie cackle every time. Scarlett chuckled, too.

It was nice to see him more relaxed. This morning after they'd woken up, he'd been on his phone scrolling through Facebook. She'd felt him stiffen beside her, and when she glanced over, she caught the headline on the sports page.

MOMENT OF TRUTH: WILL SATURDAY'S FIGHT BE THE LAST FOR BRODY "THE IRON" MINTON?

That one had been tame in comparison to some of the others that had popped up. He tried to pretend it hadn't bothered him. But it had. He'd become tense and inattentive until he got here. Ellie had brought a true smile to his face.

"She's the oldest niece, right?" Scarlett asked.

"Sure is. Just turned four, and she loves her Uncle Brody."

That had been obvious from the moment they'd arrived. Ellie had been vying since then for her uncle's attention.

"I think she's a little jealous of you. She's not used to having to share him." Elise sent her a wink.

Scarlett had picked up on that, too, and thought it was sweet. "It's a good thing I don't mind sharing then."

Elise gave an approving nod. "Anyway, the real reason I came over is Dan is about to put the steaks on. How do you like yours?"

"Medium rare."

"You're going to fit in just fine."

Happiness expanded Scarlett's chest as she watched Brody's mother walk back to her husband. She'd just gotten his mother's approval. Scarlett crossed her arms underneath her breasts and watched Brody. There was such joy on his face as he played with his niece. He'd make a great father someday.

The light feeling his mother's words had given her darkened and turned heavy. There was that kid thing again.

"How're you holding up?"

Scarlett looked over to find Tessa walking toward her, smiling. "Just taking it all in."

"I remember introducing Nick to everyone." Sadness tinged her words as she stopped beside Scarlett. She also crossed her arms and focused on her brother. "He had to go outside for a walk, to come down from the chaos."

Scarlett studied the younger woman. She'd met Tessa once, years ago, when she'd come with Brody to a concert while visiting from New York.

"I heard about the wedding. I'm sorry."

Tessa shrugged. "Love isn't always enough, you know? Sometimes you have bigger dreams that the other doesn't want to be a part of. Decisions have to be made. It sucks."

Damned if she didn't understand that herself. "It does suck."

"Nick didn't want kids. I do. Lots of them."

Children. That topic just kept coming up today.

"Making that decision had to be hard."

"It was. I love him, but I can't imagine a life without children. None of us can. We grew up in a full household."

None of us can. That one sentence hooked itself into her mind and wouldn't let go as she watched Brody sit crossed-legged on the ground and blow bubbles at a dark-haired toddler.

"What about you? Do you want kids?" There was a

probing curiosity behind her words, an interest that went further than general questioning.

"I haven't given it much thought," she evaded, not wanting to get drawn into this conversation with a woman she barely knew.

"Figured, since you were married as long as you were to Ryan and never had kids. Brody wants to have at least five."

How dare this woman make assumptions about why she hadn't had children?

"And you're telling me all this, why?" Anger vibrated her words.

"Brody has always protected me. Now it's my turn." A grim expression cast a shadow over the woman's face. "We don't usually butt into each other's business. If he gets mad, he'll get over it. Brody has never brought a woman to a family gathering. You've been married before. Never had kids. Makes a person think. I don't want him to wind up being bitch-slapped with the truth days before he's supposed to start his life with someone, like I was. Parenthood is important to him, and if it isn't to you, then you two need to have a serious talk now before either of you get any deeper into this."

Then she casually strolled away.

Motherhood had always been important to her. But she couldn't be one. Not in the biological sense. That hadn't mattered to her. It had to Ryan. It'd mattered to him so much that their infertility journey had changed him from a man she'd loved to someone she didn't know—a stranger.

What if the same thing happened with Brody? What if she was destined to repeat the past?

As much as the idea of letting Brody go killed a part of her inside, she couldn't chance being hurt like that again.

• • •

Brody scrubbed the back of his head as he watched Scarlett. Something had happened. His family could be overwhelming, but she'd been handling it pretty well, seemed to be enjoying herself. Now she sat off alone on one of the yard benches, distant and distracted.

He sat down beside her, pressing his leg into the side of hers, then nudged her with his shoulder. "What's on your mind?"

She sent him another strained smile—the fourth in the last hour. "Nothing."

That was a lie if he'd ever heard one. He needed to get her up, doing something, and out of her head.

"We're about to get a game of volleyball going? Want to join?"

Her nose scrunched. "I suck at that game. I'll just watch, if you don't mind."

"I do actually." He took her hand and tugged her to her feet.

"Brody."

"Lighten up, Scarlett. We all suck at this game."

He chanced a glance at her to make sure she hadn't been offended by the blunt comment, but she laughed softly. "All right. As long as everyone sucks, and it's not just me."

After pulling her out onto the grass and positioning her in front of the net, he took his place behind her. From the other side, Tessa volleyed the first ball. As it arced up into the air and then down toward her, Scarlett jumped up and hit it with her palm. It shot off her hand and straight into Brody's face. The unexpected sting had him bending over, clutching his nose.

"Oh my God! I told you I sucked!" She hurried over to him and rubbed his back. "Are you okay?"

Straightening, he blinked his watering eyes. "I'm fine."

"Let me see." She pulled his hand away from his nose.

"Jesus, you're bleeding. Time out, everyone."

She ignored his mumbled argument and led him into the house then into the bathroom. She lowered the lid to the toilet. "Sit."

"Scarlett, I'm fine. I've been rocked much harder in the cage. This was a baby tap that took me off guard." He looked in the mirror and pointed to his nose, where a smidge of blood surrounded one nostril. "See? It's not even really bleeding."

"I don't care. Sit."

No reason to argue with her. If it made her feel better to doctor him up, then so be it. He sat. She opened the linen closet and pulled out a burgundy washcloth. After wetting it, she wrung out the excess water then held the cold cloth to his nose.

At her tender care, warmth filled his chest. He liked having her fuss over him. He just wished she'd open up to him. "Did someone say something to you?"

She stilled, her gaze shooting up from his nose to his eyes. "Why do you ask?"

"I've known you for a long time. Something is going on in that head of yours."

She straightened, turning her attention to rinsing out the rag, her head down. "You're amazing with your nieces."

Now she was changing the subject. He sighed and raked his hand over his face, grimacing slightly as his nose tweaked at the movement. If she wasn't ready to talk about what was on her mind, then he'd give her some more time to think.

"I love spending time with Ellie."

"She's adorable." She finally twisted toward him and leaned a hip on the sink. "You'll make a great dad someday."

"I hope so. Being an uncle is a lot different than being a father. Right now, I get to rile them up and send them home, which I do every chance I get." He winked at her and was awarded an amused smile. "Do you have any nieces or nephews?"

"No. My sister hasn't married yet, and as you know, Ryan was an only child."

He nodded. "I've always been surprised that you and Ryan never had kids."

She pivoted back toward the sink and placed the damned rag in the corner. "We weren't ready for all that."

His stomach tightened. When Ryan and Scarlett first got married, all he'd talked about was having kids someday. Those conversations had died off over the last few years. Was it possible Scarlett hadn't been so on board with having kids? "Do you want kids one day?"

Her jaw clenched, and she was silent for a long, agonizing moment, then she looked him straight in the eyes. "No."

It felt like all the air had been sucked from his lungs. "None?"

"Not one. Thought I did at one time, but then I started working with kids all day."

He swallowed. Jesus. How was this even possible?

"I see," was all he could get out, his mind whirling a mile a minute.

This was why she'd grown distant throughout the day. She'd watched him play with his niece, probably freaking out about him wanting kids, just like he was freaking out about her not wanting them.

As much as he loved Scarlett, could he give up his future children to be with her?

He wasn't sure he could.

. . .

She'd never told a bigger lie.

Peeking through the blinds, Scarlett watched Brody pull away from the curb. After they'd left the cook-out, he hadn't mentioned taking her back to his place. Instead, he feigned exhaustion, saying the kids had worn him out and he wanted to hit the sack early because he had a big day of training ahead of him.

Kids had definitely exhausted him, but it wasn't from chasing them around.

Her lie had.

And she felt sick about it.

A retching came from the bathroom, and Scarlett spun around. Apparently, she wasn't the only one sick. She hurried to the bathroom then tapped on the door. "Delaney?"

"Go away. I'm dying in here."

Concerned, she chewed on her lip. Delaney hadn't been feeling well for a few days now. "I'm coming in."

As she pushed the door open, she found Delaney sitting on her knees, elbows braced on the toilet seat, forehead resting in her hands over the bowl. She groaned. "I feel like death warmed over."

"Should we go to Urgent Care?"

"No." When she glanced up, tears shone in her eyes. "I know what's wrong. I'm just too scared to confirm it."

Scarlett stared down at her best friend. "What?"

Delaney leaned over, pulled open a drawer, grabbed something wrapped in a brown paper bag and waved it toward Scarlett as she groaned again.

Scarlett took it and opened it. Her heart dropped at the pregnancy test inside. She glanced from it, back to Delaney, back to the test, and tears pricked her eyes. Everyone was getting pregnant but her.

What a horrible thing to think. She tamped down that knee jerk response—this was no time for self-pity. Her best friend needed her.

"How long have you suspected?" she asked.

"A few days," she mumbled.

"Take the test, Delaney."

Her friend lifted her head. "What if I'm right? I don't think I'm ready to face that truth yet. Right now I can still call it the mother of all stomach bugs."

"Finding out doesn't change the fact." She pulled the test from the bag and held it out. "Take it."

Delaney stared at it for a moment then hesitantly took the box. Standing, she pulled down her pajama pants. To give her a little privacy, Scarlett crumbled the bag and grabbed the discarded box, tossing them in the trash as Delaney took the test.

A few seconds later, she heard a whispered, "Oh God," and soft weeping ensued.

Scarlett didn't need to ask for the result. Delaney was pregnant. Another moment of self-pity weighed down on her. Her best friend didn't want to be pregnant, and Scarlett would've given anything to have this moment. God knew, she and Ryan had paid good money for it.

And it had never happened.

Reminding herself that this was not about her, but Delaney, she inhaled deeply and faced her friend. Still on the toilet with her pants around her ankles, Delaney had lowered her face into her hands, the positive stick pointing up to the ceiling. Her soft weeps escalated to sobs.

Scarlett hurried over and hugged her friend. "It's going to be okay."

"We used protection, Scar. I swear we did."

There was no question as to who the father was. Since her breakup, Delaney had only been with one man.

Delaney suddenly snapped her head up, her eyes wide. "I don't even know him. I'm pregnant by a man I don't even know. What the fuck, Scarlett?"

"You have options, hon," she whispered, even though her insides screamed against the alternatives that came to mind.

But this wasn't her life, it was Delaney's.

Her friend pressed her head into Scarlett's side and shook it. "No options for me other than keeping it."

"Okay. Then where do we go from here?"

"Let it digest. Make an appointment with an OB to confirm." She fell silent for a second. "Then tell Blake."

"Do you have any way to contact him?"

"Nope." Delaney gave a short laugh, straightened, and swiped at her eyes. Thankfully, it looked like the shock was wearing off. "We weren't supposed to see each other again."

"I can get Brody—"

Delaney shook her head sharply. "No go-betweens. I'll find him myself when I'm ready to tell him. It's really early still. Anything could happen. No reason to go chasing down a guy and tell him I'm pregnant only to have something happen a week from now."

"You're going to tell him, though?"

"Of course, I'm going to tell him." She slapped the stick on the corner of the sink then stood, pulling up her pants. She blew out a slow breath. "I have no idea the kind of person my baby daddy is. It's very possible he'll deny the baby is his and make this a nightmare to prove. Or he could refuse to have anything to do with us. I have to accept the possibility that I might be doing this all alone."

Scarlett wrapped her arm around her friend's shoulders. "You'll never be alone, Delaney. Aunt Scarlett will be there to help."

And just like that, she would be an aunt.

"I love you," Delaney said around another sob.

"Girl, I love you, too."

There was going to be a baby. It might not be in the way Scarlett, or even Delaney, had imagined it. But there was going to be a baby.

Chapter Eleven

Dinner tonight? I'll cook. Delaney's got a wedding shoot.

Brody reread the text, indecision warring inside him. He couldn't put her off again. This was the third text she'd sent since he'd dropped her off at her place three days ago. So far, he'd used the excuse that training had him busy—which wasn't necessarily a lie. With the fight only three days away, he was spending a lot of time in the gym. But he could afford a couple of hours to see her. He'd just needed the space to think.

All he'd succeeded in was missing her like fucking crazy.

He never thought he'd question wanting children, but he found himself wondering more than once if having nieces and nephews would be enough. If loving Scarlett would be enough. It was a vicious cycle and gave him a clearer picture of the struggle Tessa had when she'd made her decision. She'd chosen children. Brody wasn't sure if he would.

The constant whirlwind in his head made him feel like

he didn't know if he was coming or going. He was a mass of confusion. Scarlett had finally given herself over to a real relationship and had dropped a bombshell on him of epic proportions. But one thing was clear—avoiding her to collect his thoughts was not working.

Let me shower & I'll be over, he texted back.

Knowing he'd see Scarlett within the hour, he felt only excitement. Dread was nowhere on the radar. He guessed that said a lot. Maybe other people's children would be enough.

He hurried into the locker room and found Blake tying a beaten-up tennis shoe.

"Hot date?" Brody asked sarcastically.

His cousin laughed softly. "I'm going to mow Mom's yard."

"Any special bump-intos happen lately?" Blake hadn't mentioned Delaney again, so he had no idea if he'd talked to her or not.

"Nope. I've been down to the park a few times around lunch. It's like finding a needle in a haystack, man. But if I'm meant to see her, it will eventually fall into place, or I'll lose interest. Right now, I'm still interested enough to go for a walk a couple times a week." He winked at Brody as he shoved his foot into the other shoe. "What are you getting into this afternoon?"

"Scarlett's cooking me dinner."

"Awesome." He tied the laces. "Fight's in a few days."

Three.

"Yeah."

"How you feeling about it?"

Nervous as fuck.

I believe in you.

Scarlett's encouraging words immediately sprang into his mind, as they had a lot since she'd said them, especially whenever a negative headline popped up. The closer the fight came, the more he was becoming the talk of the sports industry. And damn it, the pressure of having to secure a win was getting to him, and not in a good way. For the first time in a long time, he was nervous about stepping into that cage and facing off with an opponent.

Every time his head seemed to get the best of him, when Mike was giving him a rough time, or someone questioned his future in this industry, her words were there.

And they gave him strength.

He'd never had that with a woman before. Just knowing she stood in his proverbial corner, supported him, believed in him, made him want to be the best he could be for her. That was a new feeling for him.

"I'm ready."

With Scarlett's support, he was ready for anything.

Which made the idea of letting her go so much harder.

. . .

Why was she so nervous?

Scarlett looked around the small dining room.

Table set. Check.

Candles lit. Check.

Lights dimmed. Check.

Looking killer in her new pale yellow sleeveless dress. Check.

Everything was in place. Perfectly set. But her stomach was going crazy. Brody hadn't been the same since the cookout. He hadn't sent her a nightly text since their talk, which had finally pushed her to reach out to him. Fat lot of good that had done. Though he had responded to each one, he'd been quick to decline her offers, just like he had in the past, putting distance between them when she'd still been with her ex. All she got was a lot of, *I'm really tired from training*, or, *training was brutal today, need sleep.* And so on.

Not that she should be surprised. She'd led him to believe she didn't want children, which she hadn't meant to do. It just happened. As he was asking her questions, Tessa's warning had replayed in her head, her past had roared forward, and the lie just came out then there was no taking it back. In the end, she was doing right by Brody—he wanted so much more than she'd ever be able to give him, and it was selfish of her to knowingly take him down that awful road. It was better to set him free.

She just hadn't been prepared for how she'd feel when he actually distanced himself from her.

It scared the crap out of her.

But losing him was inevitable. If not now, then in the future when he grew resentful of her infertility struggles. So far, Brody hadn't made the end of their relationship verbally official. Being the man he was, she couldn't imagine him just ghosting on her. He'd tell her to her face. So he still had to be thinking about things. She wanted to spend as much time as she could with him before then. Once he ended their relationship, she would accept it gracefully and let him go.

There. She *was* being selfish. She wanted to see him, touch him…love him.

At least for a little while longer.

The doorbell chimed. She fluffed her hair as she hurried and opened the door. Her heart skipped a beat as she took in Brody, so devilishly handsome in his jeans and T-shirt, dark hair still damp from his shower.

"Hey, sexy," she said then tilted her head up for a kiss.

"Hey, yourself." The chaste kiss he placed on her lips was quick and brief. She felt the distance widening between them. Panic squeezed her throat, but she tamped it down, reminding herself that it was the way it would have to be.

"Dinner's ready. I made a roast with potatoes, carrots, and

rice. I hope you like roast. I wasn't sure. But it was on sale, and I haven't made one in a while, so I thought what the heck." *God, shut up.* She couldn't seem to stop herself from trying to chase away any silence.

"Sounds great." He followed her into the dining room. "You really went all out with setting an atmosphere, huh?"

What did he mean by that? Did he like it? Was it too much?

Doubt dug its claws deeper into her. As they sat down, she passed the bowl of veggies to Brody, who served himself a small portion. He did the same with meat.

"Are you not hungry?" she asked.

"I have to weigh in on Friday. Right now I'm good, but I can't gorge myself like I'd want to on this fantastic meal." He sent her a smile, but there was strained edge to it.

Tension crept into her muscles, and she forced herself to relax. He had a fight in a couple of days. He was distracted. She'd already seen once how he could get distracted over a fight. She shouldn't read too much into his distance.

Dinner was still a disaster. Brody wasn't very talkative, and though she prattled on like an idiot, all she got from him were one or two word answers. By the time she had the table cleared, she was close to tears.

She walked into the living room. Brody was sprawled on the couch, with his head leaning back against the cushions, eyes closed. He *did* look exhausted. She curled up beside him and laid her head on his chest, thankful when his arm immediately went around her, his fingers playing with her shoulder.

"The next few days are going to be a bitch," he mumbled. "Weigh-in. Interviews. Training."

"Are you ready for the fight?"

"As ready as I'll ever be."

"I'd love to watch you." As soon as she said it, he stiffened underneath her.

"I can get you a ticket if you want." But he didn't sound like that was what *he* wanted.

"Next time. You have a lot going on right now. I'll just watch it on the television."

He didn't respond to that. She glanced at him—his eyes were open, and he was staring at the ceiling. Indecision pulled his usually relaxed face into hard lines.

He didn't want to be here.

"You look tired," she said.

"I'm exhausted."

"If you need to go home and get some rest, don't feel like you have to keep me entertained."

There. She'd offered the out. Would he take it? She hoped not.

"Yeah. I'm sorry, Scarlett. I think I need a really good night's sleep." He extracted himself from her and stood.

Emptiness surrounded her, physically and mentally. Not wanting him to see her hurt, she forced a happy face and accepted his kiss—another quick one.

"I usually sleep like a hibernating bear after fight. If the kid completely destroys me, you might not hear from me for a few days. I'm going to need time to accept some harsh truths about my career."

She hated the worry in his voice. Hated the fact that someone had made him doubt his ability in the cage.

"You do what you got to do." She meant that in more ways than one. "Just remember, I might not be there, but I'm in your corner, cheering you on. You've got this. I believe in you."

He stared at her a long moment. Emotions she couldn't exactly read crossed his face, but she was sure she saw sadness. And there was only one explanation for it.

The possible end of his career wasn't the only harsh truth

he was accepting.

"Good night, Scarlett," he said before he walked out of her house.

Walked out of her life. There was no doubt that she'd already lost him.

He just hadn't made it official yet.

Chapter Twelve

The jab landed hard on Brody's chin, knocking his head sideways, and his vision swam for a brief second.

Two rounds in and he'd give the kid credit—he *was* really fucking good. So good, he was worried he was going to do exactly as the newspapers had predicted and get his ass knocked out.

Brody weaved to the left, dodging another powerful throw, then countered with an uppercut. Randy's head snapped back. As he slowly lowered it, he smiled, making the bright red word KILLER visible on his mostly-black mouth guard.

"That's all you got, old man," he garbled out.

That hadn't been the only comment the kid had made throughout the fight. Randy liked to trash talk. Anytime he'd get the advantage, or took a blow from Brody, he'd toss out some smartass retort.

The purpose was to get under Brody's skin, make him angry so he'd stop fighting with his mind and just react. It was a technique he'd used once upon a time, when he'd been young and stupid, too. Now he didn't waste his energy on shit like that.

The bell rang, signaling the end of Round Two. Brody strode to his corner as Mike and the crew entered the ring. One rubbed him down, while another worked on the cut under his eye. Mike held out his latex-gloved hand under Brody's chin, waiting for him to spit his mouth guard into his palm.

"Kid's got one hell of a right," he mumbled after he took a few deep breaths.

The three-round fight had been anything but easy so far. If the match went to the judges, the scorecards would be in Randy's favor. He had to finish it this round, and he seriously worried that he wouldn't be able to.

"You need to be playing more offensively. Stay away from his fists," Mike instructed.

Brody stilled as he stared at the serious expression on his coach's face.

"You want me to dance away from him?"

"Yes. I want you to fight smart, Brody. Right now, you're not. Randy has a killer arm. He's going to knock you out if you continue to stand toe-to-toe with him. He hasn't even been dazed by one of your punches. Pick your opening. Make the landing count."

Washed up. At the end of his career. Has been. Lost his edge.

The headlines revolved around his head, festering his doubt. And Mike telling him to avoid engaging with the younger man only intensified those feelings.

That wasn't the way he fought. He was always the aggressor. It kept his opponent off-kilter. But Randy was also an aggressive fighter. So far, they had exchanged blows for the last ten minutes, Randy's having much more impact than Brody's.

As much as he hated it, he saw the wisdom in Mike's words. He finally nodded his agreement.

A loud whistle sounded. The guys quickly gathered their equipment. As Mike started to leave the cage, he clapped Brody hard on the shoulder. "Finish him."

In other words, if Brody didn't, he would lose by decision. No pressure. None at all. *Fuck.*

Once the cage was clear, he and Randy met in the middle. After tapping gloves, Brody backed off, allowing the other fighter to move into him. The action felt weird. Felt off. Every instinct had him wanting to charge his opponent, take control of the fight.

For over a minute, he avoided his opponent's advances. The crowd booed. He couldn't blame them. They'd come to see a fight, not watch two people dance around each other.

As much as he appreciated Mike's advice, he wasn't being true to himself as a fighter.

I believe in you.

Scarlett believed in him. Now he had to believe in himself, exactly like she'd told him to.

Because this was not how he fought. If it meant the end of his career, at least he'd go out on his terms, and he deserved nothing less.

Brody exploded toward Randy in a fit of quick punches and kicks, taking his opponent off-guard so he backed away. Brody spun out another high kick, his foot catching Randy on the side of the head. The kid's arms lowered and his eyes glazed over. Taking advantage of the moment, Brody landed a left hook. Randy crumbled to his knees, and Brody jumped on him, continuing an onslaught of super-fast punches to his face, locking in the knockout. The referee slid between them, waving his arms.

As he looked down at his unconscious opponent, a moment of shock buzzed through his head, muting the screaming crowd surrounding him. Holy fuck. He'd done it.

Brody raised his hands over his head. Mike and the guys ran into the cage and embraced him.

"Great job, Minton," Mike said. "We just needed to get into that kid's head."

Brody blinked at his coach, then Mike's strategy hit him. There was a reason he was the best trainer in the industry. "That's why you had me back off."

He nodded. "He was controlling that fight. You knew it. I knew it. The judges knew it. We needed to take that control back. I know what kind of fighter you are. I knew instinct would eventually win out. I'm glad I was right."

Instinct would eventually win out.

Just as Scarlett's words had given him strength when he'd needed them, Mike's knocked him hard in the gut, reminding him of the decision he had to make.

His instinct was leading him outside the cage, too. He was fighting it with everything he had, because he didn't want to let Scarlett go. He wanted to be with her.

But sometimes that wasn't enough. She was a source of strength he never expected, and she was also going to be his eventual downfall. Because for the first time, he might settle for less than he deserved, just to be with her.

Randy walked over to him, interrupting his thoughts. The man lifted his now ungloved hand, and Brody took it. "Great fight, man. I look forward to our next match, because I'll be gunning for you."

Brody grinned. It'd been a hard fight, but he had shut up the naysayers, reminded everyone here that he was still a force to be reckoned with—exactly like Scarlett said he would be. "You can try."

The other fighter smiled then moved off to the side of the cage to do his interview about his loss.

Brody had a microphone thrust in his face, too, and his

focus was diverted to the slew of questions, and away from what he'd do about his problems at home.

• • •

Brody slipped into his Mercedes and groaned. His muscles screamed in agony and would for the next few days, just like they always did right after a tough fight. Greg did have a hell of a fighter on his roster now, and the kid would have a great future in CMC.

But tonight it had been an old man's moment.

Mike was already working to schedule a contention fight. After all these years, Brody had finally advanced up the MMA ladder. He should be ecstatic, but as the night wore on, his thoughts kept turning to Scarlett and his coach's after-fight words.

Instinct told him he'd want children and would never be truly happy without that option. But his heart was killing him with the love he had for Scarlett.

A sharp beep came from inside the glove compartment, signaling he'd missed either a call or text. He always left his phone in the car before a fight because he didn't need any distractions while trying to get into his fighter's mindset. Opening the compartment, he grabbed his cell, flicked his thumb across the screen, and tapped the text notification from his oldest sister.

Call me as soon as you get out. Don't care how late.

Concern grabbed him by the neck, and he immediately pressed the phone icon to connect with Savannah.

His sister never texted this late, and she sure as fuck didn't tell him to call her.

"Hey," she breathed.

"What's the matter?"

There was a deep inhale. "Ellie saw the fight." Before he could respond, she quickly added, "I didn't know. I'd put her to bed like I usually do before your fight, and then Stan and I settled in on the couch to watch. Ellie sat at the top of the stairs."

Closing his eyes, he leaned his head back and groaned. That hadn't been a bloodless match. He could only imagine what the four-year-old was thinking. "Is she okay?"

"No. She's been crying since Boss knocked you down and busted open that place on your cheek. She won't believe me when I told you were fine."

"Did you have her watch the interviews after the fight?"

"She refuses to come out of her room."

"Let me talk to her."

A few seconds passed before he heard Savannah say, "Ellie. Uncle Brody is on the phone. He wants to talk to you."

A wail followed, growing louder as either Savannah held the phone to Ellie's ear, or the child took the phone.

"Hey, princess."

The crying only intensified. Brody's gut clenched tight at his niece's distress. The sound lessened just a little, and then Savannah was back on the line. "She pushed the phone away. I don't know what to do right now."

"Do I need to come over?"

"I hate to ask you to. I know how tired you are after a fight, but she's a mess. I think she needs to see you in person."

She didn't have to ask twice. "Give me twenty minutes."

"Thank you, Brody."

"Don't mention it." He ended the call. Yeah, he was dog-assed tired, but he sure as hell wasn't going to let his niece worry herself sick over him.

Since it was almost one thirty in the morning, traffic was light and it only took him ten minutes to get to his sister's house. He hurried up the cobblestone walkway. Savannah opened the door before he reached the porch and stepped back as he walked into the house, "She's upstairs in her room."

Knowing his face was all banged up, he hesitated. After a fight, he tended to stay away from the kids for a week or two. They'd seen him with faded bruises, understood that he "wrestled" for his job, but they'd never seen him fresh from the cage. He circled his face with his finger. "Is this going to make it worse?"

Savannah held up her hands helplessly. "I don't know."

Well, if she was willing to chance it, so was he. He took the steps two at a time, then slowed right outside Ellie's door, peeking in. If she'd fallen asleep, he wasn't sure he should wake her. But she was laying in the middle of her pink, plastic toddler bed, clutching her dolly with her thumb in her mouth, her cheeks still wet from crying. Ellie only sucked her thumb when she was upset.

As he stepped inside, he tapped on the door. Her eyes flicked to the door, and then she threw back her princess blanket and jumped out of bed. "Uncle Brody!"

She flew across the room and tossed herself into his arms. He smothered a grunt of pain as he hoisted her up on his side. "How are you, princess?"

She didn't seem to hear his question—her gaze was glued to the wound on his upper cheek, her cherub face pinched in concern. She placed her tiny hand on his temple beside the gash.

"Ouchy," she said.

His heart swelled to busting. "Yeah. Uncle Brody has an ouchy."

"That man hurt you."

He carried her over to the bed and placed her on the mattress. After tucking the covers back around her, he squatted beside her and took her hand in his. "You remember how Uncle Brody gets ouchies a lot?"

She nodded.

"You remember what you saw on the TV?"

Fear came into her eyes, but she nodded again a little more fiercely.

"Well, Uncle Brody gets his ouchies from doing that. It's his job, like how your daddy's job is—"

"Playing in the dirt," she interrupted.

Brody chuckled. "Yeah, playing in dirt."

Stan was a landscaper. He came home dirty every day.

"You be okay?"

"Yes, I'll be okay."

Accepting the simple answer, she nestled farther into her covers then turned to her side, her eyelids growing heavy.

"Love you," she whispered as her eyes closed.

A loving pain grew in his chest as he leaned over and kissed the top of her head, "I love you, too, princess."

As he stood, he gazed down at his niece. His coach's words, the overwhelming love he had for this child, were a message to him—signs he had to listen to no matter how hard it hurt.

Not having children wasn't a possibility. Not for him. He couldn't imagine missing this.

He loved Scarlett. Had for a very long time. Had never been able to move on from her. Maybe this had to happen so he could.

Even though letting her go was the last thing he wanted to do, they wanted a different future.

There was no coming back from that.

• • •

Two days later, Brody sat outside Delaney's home in his car, staring at the front door.

Could he go through with this?

Other than a reply to her congratulatory text saying how

proud she was of him, he hadn't spoken to Scarlett. She'd taken his words to heart the night they'd had dinner together and given him the space to rest that he'd requested. She had no idea that he'd spent the last two days trying to figure out how he was going to tell her their relationship was over.

In theory, it shouldn't be hard. Just say it. But the reality was, even though he knew this was the right decision for both of them, his heart wasn't in it.

Today he had to pull the Band-Aid off, for both their sakes. Once it was done, it was done, and they both could start the healing process.

It was going to take him a while to do that. He'd loved this woman for so long. She filled a place in him that had been empty. But being with her meant he'd have to let go of his dreams—his future children.

Tessa had walked away the night before her wedding because of a decision like this.

And he had to walk away from Scarlett.

He never imagined it would be him ending things. For now, he could be happy with her, but instinct told him that years down the road he'd grow resentful. Neither of them deserved that.

He opened the car door then walked up the path and tapped on the door. Seconds later, Scarlett answered, wearing a pair of overly large Superman pajamas and a red cami. Pain sliced across his chest, and he fisted his hands to keep from rubbing the area.

His heart would have him make a decision that would doom them to failure. He couldn't listen to it.

"Brody!" Scarlett jerked slightly in surprise. "I wasn't expecting you."

"We need to talk."

Her throat worked, but she nodded and stepped back, allowing him in. "Ah. The 'we need to talk' talk. Can't wait."

As he entered, he saw Delaney sitting curled up in the corner of the couch, wrapped in a blanket, wads of tissues surrounding her. A movie was paused on the TV. She turned to look at her with bloodshot eyes.

He froze. "I'm interrupting."

Delaney jumped off the couch. "No. You're fine. I'll go to my room."

She was gone just like that.

"Is she okay?" he asked.

Scarlett stared after her friend. "She will be."

She turned her attention back on him. There was a distance in her eyes that hadn't been there before, like she already knew what was about to happen. "We needed to talk?"

After she closed the door, she crossed her arms protectively around her middle. He hated that he was the cause of that protective stance. Hated he would be just another man who'd hurt her.

Better the hurt now, before they both got in too deep.

Who was he kidding? He already was. At least Scarlett was in the beginning stages—she'd be able to move on a lot faster than he would.

"I can't continue this," he said, his throat clenched tight.

It was out. He'd said it. And he instantly wanted to take it back. But he couldn't. He knew himself.

She nodded again, then looked down at her feet. "I've been waiting for this. I've noticed you distancing yourself since we had that talk at your sister's house."

So it had been something that had been bothering her, too.

"I'm sorry, Scarlett."

She waved away his words. "Don't apologize for being honest with yourself, Brody." Finally, she glanced up, a strained smile on her lips. "No reason to waste your time with something that will never be more than what it is right now. I get it."

He recoiled from her words. "Don't put it that way. None of the time I've spent with you has been wasted."

She remained silent for a moment. "You know what I mean. There's no future here. I knew it that day at the cook-out. I just didn't want to let go. Thank you for being strong enough to do it for us."

He didn't feel strong, he felt weak. He was seconds away from saying "fuck it" and damn the consequences. He'd faced some of the best in the industry and leaving this woman was more painful than anything that had happened to him in the cage.

"You're going to be a great father one day," she added.

It was the reminder he needed of why he was doing this. He needed to get out of here before he did something that would only make it worse on both of them.

"I'll go now." Without even looking at her, he strode out of the house, leaving his heart behind him. He could only hope that it would find its way back home one day.

• • •

Scarlett closed the door and laid her head on the cool wood. "I'll miss you," she whispered.

Her vision swam, and she allowed the tears to fall free. All the fight had left her.

She'd known this moment was coming. With her "confession," she'd made certain Brody would leave her, and it had to be his decision to end the relationship. If she'd been the one, it would've been harder for Brody to move on.

She didn't want that for him. She wanted him to have everything he desired—including kids. She'd saved him from years of heartache, from growing to resent her, and that would certainly happen. More failed IVFs with donor eggs. Surrogacies gone wrong. Adoptions fallen-through.

She may never be a mother.

And she'd be damned if Brody would never be a father.

The reminder didn't help the pain slicing her heart in two. After everything she'd sworn not to do, she'd fallen hard for that man. And now she was doing right by him—letting him go to have the future he wanted.

Soft footsteps sounded behind her, and Scarlett pushed off the door then glanced at Delaney, who was still wrapped in her blanket, eyes bright red. She'd gotten confirmation today. Nine weeks pregnant. Now she was struggling with how to tell Blake, how he would react, and if she would be having the baby alone. She'd find out soon, though. Earlier, she'd said she would make that huge step within the next week or two. Then who knew what would happen. Her future was just as uncertain as Scarlett's was.

Strange how both of their lives were being turned upside down over children.

"You okay?" she asked.

"No." Tears blurred her vision again.

Answering grief sprang to her friend's eyes. "Come on, then. Let's throw our pity party with Gerard Butler."

Delaney wrapped her arm around Scarlett's shoulders, and they both shuffled toward the couch.

She just had to keep reminding herself that she'd done the right thing.

Or else she was liable to do something stupid, like not give a damn about what Brody wanted and try to have a future with him anyway.

How selfish would that be?

Chapter Thirteen

Scarlett watched the two burly men carry the couch to the moving truck. A few days ago, Ryan had contacted her, saying she needed to get what she wanted out of the house. Monica was moving in and wanted Scarlett's stuff gone before then.

Finding out Ryan was moving his girlfriend into what used to be their home hadn't caused the slightest ache. Missing Brody was using up all her pain. It'd been a week since he'd ended their relationship. A long, agonizingly painful week, so miserable that she'd come damn close to picking up the phone and telling him she'd lied about the whole thing.

She wanted children. Desperately. She just couldn't have them. Then, and only then, did her failed marriage come to mind, reminding her that love wasn't always enough.

Tires sounded behind her, and she twisted to look. Her heart dropped as she watched the white Dodge Durango pull into the driveway and park.

Why was Ryan here?

He sat behind the wheel for a few moments, rubbing his hands over his eyes. Finally, he opened the door and climbed out, confusion on his face as he looked from her to the moving van.

Slowly, his expression melted into realization. "Jesus. You were getting your stuff to put into storage today. I'm sorry. I forgot." The entire time he spoke, he avoided looking directly at her. "I'll stay out of the way."

She'd been married to the man long enough to know his agitation meant he was upset about something.

"Ryan?" she asked.

Swollen red eyes met hers. She pressed her hand to her mouth, dread clenching her throat. The entire time they were together, Ryan had only cried twice—both times their IVFs had failed.

The baby.

"Is everything okay?" It was a stupid question. Obviously everything wasn't okay, but it was the only thing she could think to say.

Turning his head away, he rubbed the back of his head. "Monica lost the baby." His voice cracked on the last word.

Air punched out of her mouth. All she felt was sorrow for both of them. As much as it'd hurt having Ryan get another woman pregnant, losing the child was something she'd never wished on him. He'd already had enough hopes killed with her to fill a lifetime.

"I'm so sorry, Ryan."

He bowed his head as his shoulders began to shake. "I just want to be a dad."

She wasn't sure what to do or say. She was the soon-to-be ex-wife. Her husband was talking about the woman he cheated with and made a baby. But one thing was for certain—she couldn't ignore his pain.

"I left the coffeemaker. Want a cup?"

His head slowly turned back toward her, then he nodded. Without waiting for him to follow, she started walking toward the open front door. His footsteps sounded behind her. She stepped into the house that had been her home for the last four years. The living room had been wiped clean except for the rug Ryan had picked out and the huge sixty-inch flat screen he'd bought. She'd taken the smaller one from the bedroom.

He didn't have any kind of reaction to what she'd taken. Most likely he didn't give a crap right now.

After walking into the country kitchen, she placed a coffee filter in the machine then added the grounds and water.

A stool being pulled out scraped against the wood floor. When she turned, she found him perched on the edge of one with his elbows up on the island, head cradled in his palm. He looked so dejected. She hurt for him.

"When?" she asked.

"Early this morning. We just left the hospital. She was so upset afterward she told me to leave her alone. I didn't want to leave her." Then he glanced up with a stricken expression. "I'm sorry. I shouldn't be talking to you about this."

"It's fine." And it really was. She felt nothing but sadness for her ex. Maybe it had to do with the fact their marriage had been over long before it was official. Though there would always be a hurt from the things he'd said to her, the anger was gone.

A tense silence fell between them before he said, "I owe you an apology."

His admission startled her. Yeah, he did, for a lot of things, but one, Ryan never apologized, and two, she wasn't sure which grievance he was referring to.

"I punished you for something you couldn't help. I just wanted a child so badly. The more we tried, the angrier and more resentful of you I got."

She'd known that. She'd felt some of it herself toward him, especially when he'd put his foot down and said they weren't going to try anymore.

"We had options, Ryan. If you wanted to be a dad so badly why did you refuse them?"

Silence greeted her question, then he lifted his arms. "I couldn't handle another heartbreak."

And yet, here he was again. Except this time, there had been a baby and not just the hope of one. That was damn sad.

"We'd already tried in-vitro twice," he continued. "Everything was so clinical. Charting. Pills. Injections. Jacking off in a cup. It was so exhausting. The disappointment changed me. By the time we realized you couldn't have children, I was full of so much sadness and anger the mere idea of prolonging the process filled me with bitter anxiety. Instead, I turned those emotions on you."

She stared at her ex. This was the first time he had truly opened up about his reasoning behind not wanting to continue their infertility journey. "We could've adopted, Ryan."

"And what?" he asked, piercing with his eyes. "Spend years trying to adopt only to have the mother decide she wants to keep the baby at the last minute? We take the baby home, and she decides two months later she made a mistake? I couldn't invite more of that in my life." He stared off into the distance. "Maybe I'm being punished now for the way I treated you the last couple of years."

"Don't think like that. Miscarriages happen."

His shoulders slumped. "I was finally going to be a dad."

"And you still can be." She paused. "Do you love her?"

He eyed her for a doubtful moment before saying, "Yes, I do."

"Then don't make the same mistakes with her that you made with me. You should be with her right now."

"She doesn't—"

"I said the same thing, remember? But I needed you. We needed to grieve together. We didn't. We allowed resentment and bitterness to create distance between us. She's in pain right now. You are, too. You should be together."

"How can you stand there and do that?" There was no censure in his voice, just a tinge of awe.

"Our marriage was over long before you cheated, Ryan. Honestly, looking back, I think it was over after the second in-vitro failed, and we had different opinions on how to proceed. You were done. I wanted to continue trying. That made you angry at me, and I was angry at you for giving up. We only stuck it out as long as we did because we didn't know how to end it. We'd gotten so caught up in our own emotions that we allowed ourselves to just roll through the last couple of years. It wasn't healthy."

A small smile came to his lips, and he shook his head. "That's the Scarlett I remember. Not the depressed, beat-down woman you became. Brody's good for you."

At the mention of his name, her heart skipped a beat. "How do you know about Brody?"

"I put two-and-two together when he knocked me a good one in the grill."

Her mouth popped open. "He did? When?"

"Right after he got back from the Bahamas."

And that was why it was finally okay for him to pursue her. He'd ended his friendship with Ryan—over her. "Unfortunately, he broke things off with me a few days ago."

"What?" Ryan shook his head. "That's…shocking."

"Why?"

"I suspected he had feelings for you."

"You did?"

"Not right away, mind you. In fact, it wasn't until he stopped hanging around here last year that it sort of clicked for me. He wasn't any busier than usual, but he was adamant about not hanging around here or with you."

So that confirmed his interest in her had been the

motivation behind his absence. It made sense with the way he was in the Bahamas, and his determination to keep her at arm's length.

"What happened?" Ryan asked.

It was hard to believe she was sitting here having this conversation with her ex, but if there was anyone who would understand, he would. He'd been through it with her. "He wants children."

"So? You do, too."

"He wants a houseful of kids."

"I still don't get it, Scarlett."

"You saw what happened to us because of my infertility. We didn't know about it when we got married. I know now. Why would I put Brody through that?"

"Does he know the truth?"

She swallowed. "No. He thinks I don't want kids."

Sighing, he shook his head. "You owe him the truth."

"Why? So he can grow to resent me, too?"

Ryan flinched from her words. "Damn. I did a number on you, didn't I?" He rubbed his forehead. "Fuck. I'm sorry, Scarlett. Brody is not me, though."

No. Brody wasn't.

"I handled our infertility horribly," he continued. "But our situation was different. Like you said, we didn't know. We went through a lot of heartache that neither of us handled well. We didn't know how to support each other. We grew, or I grew, resentful. I blamed you. With Brody, he'll know from the get-go that it won't be conventional or easy."

She bit her lip. He had a point.

"Believe it or not, I *want* you to be happy, Scarlett. I went about finding my happiness the wrong way, I'll admit that. But I have found it all the same. I feel the best I have in years." He grimaced. "I hope being open about that doesn't hurt you."

"No." She shook her head. "I get what you're saying.

Brody has helped bring me back to life, too."

"Then why would you take the coward's way out and allow him to believe a lie? If it's not going to work between you two, it should be because of the truth. Not lies. Trust me on that. I should've been honest with you, and I made everything worse because I wasn't." He slipped off the stool. "Anyway, I'm going to Monica."

"Good," she mumbled, distracted by Ryan's speech.

He stopped at the kitchen door and looked over his shoulder. "I wish you much happiness, Scarlett."

Their eyes meet. They had no reason to stay in contact. They'd just cleared the air. Nothing was connecting them any longer. He'd sign the divorce papers and put them back in the mail. This was good-bye. "I wish the same for you."

Ryan nodded then left the kitchen. Crossing her arms, she stood in the house that hadn't been a home for a very long time and felt the weight of the last few years lift. She never imagined coming face-to-face with her ex would be the final moment she needed to completely move on from the pain from the past.

But she was ready.

And if Brody was going to leave her, it would be because he knew everything.

• • •

Scarlett rubbed her sweaty hands together as she approached the front door. She'd tried calling and texting Brody over the last couple of days to get him to meet with her so they could talk. Her attempts went unanswered. Frustrated, she'd gone to his place last night, but her knock didn't get her desired outcome. She finally received a text, though. One that had punched her hard in the gut.

The text had simply said, "*I can't, Scarlett.*"

She'd come damn close to just telling him the truth over text, but she stopped herself from doing that. He deserved to have her look him in the face when she told him everything, though going about it this way might not have been the best option, either. She stared at Savannah's door. It was Sunday. The Minton Family gathering day. His bike was parked out front. He was here. His *entire* family was here.

He couldn't avoid her here.

Maybe she should just track him down at the gym? Immediately, she shook away that thought. Doing this in front of his family was bad enough; she refused to do it in front of other men.

She knocked on the door. Fight or flight kicked in, flight winning, and she spun away from the door.

But she loved Brody. It was past time she fought to keep him. She forced herself to turn back to the door as it opened.

Tessa's eyes widened as they latched onto Scarlett. "Whoa. Brody's going to be shocked to see you. The entire family is."

So they all knew. She guessed that made it easier.

"What are you doing here?" Tessa asked, crossing her arms.

She studied the younger woman who had feisty little sister written all over her. "I'd like to see Brody."

"Just leave him alone, okay? The decision was hard enough without you having second thoughts and making it worse."

The verbal smack down stung, causing her anger to spike. This woman had butted her nose into their business from the moment Brody had brought her to meet the family. Enough was enough. "Did Brody go all bulldog and refuse to let Nick see you?"

The woman flinched back. "I'm trying to save him from the same heartache I'm going through." She stepped out onto the porch, closing the door behind her. "Do you have any idea how hard it is to be in love with someone you don't have a future with? Do you have any idea how hard it is to look that person in the face and let them go, even with them pleading for you to stay? I do. And Brody isn't going to. You need to leave."

"Not until I speak to Brody."

"Why?" Tessa raised her arms and shook them. "You don't want children. Brody does. What more is there to talk about? Why do you want to make this harder?"

It all snapped into place for her. Tessa wasn't just protecting her brother. She had some kind of unresolved emotions toward her ex-fiancé, and Scarlett was the perfect target for everything she was keeping bottled up.

"I'm sorry your situation with Nick has sucked, but I'm not him, and Brody is not you. This is *our* relationship. Not yours. You need to let me see him."

Tessa snapped her mouth shut as her body went rigid. She fisted her hands into tight balls, then promptly burst into uncontrollable sobs. At the woman's obvious anguish, Scarlett wrapped her arm around her shoulders. "I'm so sorry."

Tessa pressed her face into Scarlett's shoulder, and she wondered if Brody's sister had truly cried for her loss yet, or if she'd kept it all bottled up inside and was finally exploding.

"Brody doesn't deserve this pain," she wept between clenched teeth. "Don't continue to hurt him."

"I don't want to hurt him. I love him."

"You love me?"

The unexpected male voice made both women stiffen. Scarlett released Tessa and turned to find Brody standing directly behind them, an unreadable expression on his face. Scarlett swallowed. "Yes, I love you."

He just continued to stare at her, guarded and distant. Whatever he'd been feeling toward her had not been moved by her declaration of love. If anything, she may have made things even worse.

"Just leave him alone," Tessa cried out. "Can't you see he's made his decision?"

Brody's gaze snapped to her. "Tessa, stay out of it."

Her brother's reprimand made the woman jerk straight as if he'd slapped her. She stared at Brody, who never relaxed his stiff posture as he held her gaze. Again bursting into tears, she shoved past him and into the house.

"I'm sorry about my sister's display." He worked his neck back and forth. "Nick won't leave her alone. He's convinced that he'll eventually wear her down so she'll come back to him. If he shows back up while I'm here, I'm going to fucking punch him in the face. She can't take much more from him."

That was sad.

"Why are you here, Scarlett? Tessa was right. I *have* made my decision, and I don't see how us continuing on is good for either one of us."

"We needed to talk."

"I think we've said everything we can about the subject."

Scarlett gnawed on her lower lip. There wasn't a crack, no give, in his armor anywhere. He was protecting himself. He was preparing, just like Tessa had done with her ex, to turn her away, no matter what he felt for Scarlett.

Because he was putting his happiness first. She envied him for that, wished she'd done the same. Though, if she had, they might never have had this time together.

That, she'd never regret.

What she did regret was the lie she'd told to protect herself. She hadn't done it for her happiness, she'd done it out of fear. And she was done with being afraid.

"I lied to you," she blurted.

Brody's arms slowly lowered to his sides, shock evident on his face. "About what?"

"I do want kids."

Closing his eyes, he heaved a loud sigh then turned toward the house. "I can't do this, Scarlett. You've already said you don't want kids, you can't take that back just because we're aren't together anymore."

He was walking away from her, convinced this was some kind of ploy to get him back. She'd created this mess. Now she had to fix it. Stepping toward his retreating back, she held out her hands. "I can't *have* kids."

Brody froze. Not a muscle moved, nor did he speak a word.

The silence weighed heavy on her, and she swallowed. She hated being vulnerable, revealing her darkest secret. One marriage had already been ruined because of it—she wasn't sure how she'd handle it if Brody chose not to be with her because of it.

"You can't have kids?" he asked with his back still to her.

"Not in the biological sense, anyway."

"So you lied to push me away?"

"I lied to protect myself," she answered honestly. "The day of the cook-out I knew I couldn't give you what you wanted."

He finally faced her, his expression an impenetrable mask, giving her nothing as to where his thoughts were. Right now, she was dealing with the fighter, not the man. He wasn't going to give her an inch until he was ready to do so.

"What I wanted was you and the possibility of a future," he said. "But you decided that I didn't get a say in that, and lied to me." He sucked on his teeth, showing the first visible sign of anger. "I agonized over that decision, Scarlett. Leaving you was the hardest goddamn thing I've ever done, and you're telling me it was a *lie*." He shouted the last word, causing her to flinch.

"Yes."

He shoved a hand through his hair as he paced the porch, his armor obliterated now. "Jesus. Christ. What kind of man do you think I am? Do you really believe I'd stop loving you because of something you have no control over?"

"My husband did," she whispered.

Again Brody froze. "What did you say?"

"Our problems started four years ago when we decided we were ready to have children. One year we wasted trying to do it naturally. Then we started the testing. They couldn't find any known reason, so we tried a couple of intrauterine cycles of fertility treatments. Those didn't work. So we moved on to in-vitro. We did it twice. Neither batch produced any viable embryos. I never even got to do the two-week wait."

Brody stared at her with an intense look. "Ryan stopped loving you because you're infertile?"

"No. The emotions bled from us trying to have a baby and failing over and over again. We both changed. He just got mean. I got depressed. We grew farther and farther apart."

He lowered into a wicker rocking chair. "And you didn't want to repeat history."

She sat in the chair beside his. "You want children so badly, Brody. It may never happen if you're with me. I was terrified that you'd grow to resent me."

He frowned at her. "I'd never resent you for something like that."

"Brody—"

He waved at her. "This is a lot to process, Scarlett. I'm hurt that you lied to me—thought me capable of being such a dickhead. I need to think."

Tears burned the back of her eyes; she blinked them away and nodded. "I understand. I'll give you space."

She stood up and walked down the stairs, and he didn't try to stop her. Nor did he say a word as she slipped behind the wheel of her car. As she pulled back onto the road, she let the tears fall. She'd said she loved him. Brody hadn't returned the sentiment. He was never going to forgive her.

And she had no one to blame but herself.

. . .

A whirring was all Brody heard as he stepped back into the house. Scarlett had told him so much he was having a hard time processing it all.

She wanted kids, but had lied to him about it.

It changed everything, yet nothing, because she hadn't trusted him enough to tell him the truth.

He glanced upstairs. He'd been harsh to Tessa and needed to go apologize. He hurried up the steps and found her in her room, sitting in the window, knees hugged to her chest, as she stared out into the front yard.

"She left," Tessa said. "I take it her guilt trip didn't work?"

Tessa had been a ball of anger the last few days, snapping at everyone or anyone within an inch of her. Savannah had threatened to make her go live with their parents if she didn't adjust her attitude.

"There wasn't a guilt trip. She told me the truth."

"What? That she wants kids?"

After two failed attempts at getting Tessa to change her mind about having a family, Nick had then worked the angle that he'd just been joking. He wanted kids, too. Desperation to win back the woman he loved might make him willing to go along with the kids route, but Tessa knew how he really felt now and refused to come back. It was a no-win situation for both of them.

"Not exactly. She let me know she can't have kids. She and Ryan had tried for years. Had two failed IVF procedures."

"*What*?" Her head snapped in his direction, eyes huge. As she lowered her face into her palms, she repeated, "Oh, God."

His sister's reaction confused the shit out of him. "What's the matter with you?"

As she lifted her head, a tear leaked from the corner of her eye. "I had no idea. I was so focused on my issues that I didn't even stop to think there was another reason."

"Tessa, what the fuck are you talking about?"

"At the cook-out, I told her how much you wanted kids. Made it clear that you'd never be happy without them. Told her if she didn't plan on kids, she needed to walk away from you."

Stunned, he could only stare at his sister, his ability to speak completely shut off. That explained Scarlett's one-eighty change that day, the out-of-the-blue conversation about children, why she had started acting so damn weird.

A flood of emotions hit him at once. "That was none of your business. Jesus. Fucking. Christ. If you'd kept your damn mouth shut, Scarlett and I wouldn't have even been talking about kids yet. Instead, she felt pressured into ending things prematurely because of you. You fed her insecurities. Goddammit, Tessa." He waved his hand toward the window. "And I just let her leave. She told me she loved me, and I let her leave."

"Brody, I'm sorry. I thought I was helping you. I messed it all up instead." She began to cry again.

Tears. Fucking tears. He hated seeing his sister cry, and took a calming breath, trying to control his rolling fury. He could strangle her right now, but Tessa would never intentionally hurt him. "Yeah. You did. Now I have to fix it."

• • •

"I don't want to talk about it, Scarlett," Delaney muttered as she shoved the lens into her camera case, getting ready to go out on a shoot.

"That's what you've been saying for two weeks. You need to talk about it."

Delaney's head snapped up. The anger pinching her lips took Scarlett aback. "Listen, when you have to tell a virtual stranger that you're pregnant with his child, then you can tell me what I need. Right now, I need you to back the hell off me."

She'd watched Delaney go through a wide range of emotions since she'd gotten confirmation from the OB/GYN. Sadness, panic, rage, numbness. She talked about all of those feelings, her worries, her fears, but the one thing she'd neglected to talk about since vowing to tell the father of her baby, *was* the father of the baby.

"The longer you put this off, the harder it's going to be," Scarlett insisted, refusing to back down.

Delaney slung the strap over her shoulder, straightened, then slammed both fists onto her hips. "I bumped into him yesterday at the park while I was taking pictures. He wants to grab coffee or something. So I'm in contact with him. Now back off, okay? You have no idea what's going on in my head."

She held up her hands. "All right. I'm backing."

"Thank you," Delaney said. "Now I've got to go. I'm already running late."

Without another word, she spun and stormed out of the house. The door slammed shut behind her. Scarlett flinched. The only other time Delaney had been this closed off was when she'd been in that relationship with the dickhead. All Scarlett wanted to do was help.

Seemed like she couldn't do anything right anymore.

She lowered herself to the couch then looked at her phone lying face up on the coffee table, something she'd been doing a lot of the last five days. It stayed silent. Never rang. Never beeped.

At all.

She had no family and no Brody.

With things so tense between her and Delaney, she felt

isolated. She thought she'd felt alone in her marriage, but this was worse, because she had ruined her one true chance at happiness.

Out of fear.

Brody's silence was slowly killing her inside, but she had to respect his space and the implication of his silence—that he couldn't forgive her. She'd been the one who'd lied. Her reasoning didn't matter. She'd hurt him by not believing in him.

Believing in *them*.

A knock came at the door. She jumped, then hurried to answer it. Her heart clenched tight at Brody standing there, his dark hair combed back. Then her gaze fell on the tiny white puffball cradled in the crook of his tattooed, muscular arm.

She lifted her questioning eyes to his as he held out the kitten.

"This is Prince."

Mind racing, she took the kitten, smiling at its sweet cries. "Nice to meet you, Prince."

"I thought I'd introduce him to his mother."

Her gaze shot from the tiny pointed ears up to his eyes. "His what?"

"He's yours. But he's going to want to come play with his sister some, you know, until we figure out the living arrangements."

She opened her mouth, closed it, then opened it again. "I don't understand."

"He's not from the same mom and dad as Princess, but that doesn't matter. They'll be family anyway."

Confused, she stared at him. "So, you want me to bring Prince to play with Princess every so often?"

"I'm botching this horribly." He grimaced. "The cat is a symbol, Scarlett."

"A symbol?"

He exhaled roughly. "For families. You know, you don't have to be blood to be related." He brushed his hand down his face. "This went so differently in my head."

Fighting a smile, she asked, "How did it go in your head?"

"I'd give you the cat, tell you that Princess was his sister, and you'd miraculously put two-and-two together and see I was telling you that I don't care if we never have biological children of our own. I don't care if it's a litter of cats we call our kids, we will be parents in some way."

Tears burned the back of her eyes. "I'm not trying to harp, Brody, but do you truly understand what you're signing up for? I know we are nowhere near even discussing having kids, but one day, that will be a topic. There's a lot of heartbreak that comes with it. I've experienced it. You haven't. I don't want you to regret this moment."

He stepped forward and took her face between his palms. "I know I love you." Her heart skipped a beat, but before she could say anything, he continued. "Yes, I want kids one day, and I understand that it's going to be an uphill fight, but I accept that fight as mine as well." His thumb caressed her cheek. "You have no idea, but you gave me strength when I was weak. I won that fight by remembering that you believed in me, you stood in my corner. Now I want the chance to stand in yours. Be *your* strength when you are weak."

She smiled through her tears. "I love you, too. I can't think of anyone I'd rather co-parent two gorgeous kitties with."

"We can face anything as long as it's together. I believe that."

She cupped his cheek. "I believe in *us*."

Epilogue

She was one lucky woman.

Scarlett's heart swelled to bursting as Brody took his place beside his comic book hero, Stan Lee, with the biggest grin she'd ever seen on his face. Brody clasped the writer's hand in an eager handshake, then the photographer and Scarlett snapped a picture. They'd arrived at Dragon*Con last night. Everything about the convention had surpassed her expectations. The mass quantity of people was almost overwhelming, but she couldn't think of another place she'd rather be than here with the man she loved.

Mr. Lee patted Brody on the shoulder, said something, and then Brody walked over to her all starry-eyed. He placed his hand on his chest and sighed dramatically. "Stan Lee touched me."

"Shut up," Scarlett said with a laugh, knowing he was poking fun at her reaction to meeting Norman Reedus a few months ago.

As he came to stand beside her, he dropped his arm across her shoulders and pulled her to his side, placing a hard kiss on the top of her head. "That was fucking *awesome*, Miss Packard. Thank you."

Miss Packard.

An immediate grin came to her lips. She loved the sound of her maiden name coming from his mouth. Yesterday, she'd officially and legally won her name back. Finalization of her divorce had been the last loose string from her past that she'd needed to tie off. All the *i*'s had been dotted, the *t*'s crossed and everything was filed with the courts.

Now she was truly free to have a future with Brody.

She leaned her head back and was rewarded with a quick kiss there, too. "I love to make you smile."

"You do. Every single day."

He did the same for her. After years of anguish, she was finally truly, deeply, happy.

"So what do you want to get into next?" he asked.

"I saw *The Originals* cast are here, and they have a panel later. We might want to get in line now."

An exaggerated pained grimace crossed his face. "*The Originals*, really?"

"Hey," she lightly pinched his side. "You get Stan Lee, I get Elijah Mikaelson."

He laughed. "I don't care where I go as long as I'm with you."

That sentence summed up their relationship perfectly. Obstacles would definitely pop up in the future, but with Brody by her side, it didn't matter where the road led them, they'd face it together.

Brody had become *her* best friend, her confidante, her support.

Her heart had been healed by this man's love. And she had a life full of hope to look forward to.

Acknowledgments

A part of me fell in love with Brody "The Iron" Minton the moment he showed up at the veterinary clinic holding a white puffball kitty named Princess, in *Fighting Love*. And I kept falling deeper in love as the story progressed. Who couldn't fall for kid-loving, kitty-owning, confident-as-hell MMA fighter alpha male?

Readers felt the same. We *loved* Brody Minton.

After finishing *Fighting Love*, I never had any doubt that I would eventually write Brody's story. It just took me a while to get to it.

Thank you to the readers for loving Brody as much as I did.

I also want to thank Entangled Publishing for taking on three more "Love to the Extreme" books, so Brody could be brought to life.

Thank you to Liz Pelletier and Robin Haseltine for their superb editing. You guys know exactly what need to be added to bring my books to the next level. I love working with you two.

On the personal side...

I want to thank my partner in life, Ron, for lending me his ear as I go into freak-out mode when I'm stuck in a corner. This man not only listens, but he provides awesome ideas that spark my creativity. I'm giving him credit for helping me with the ending of this book *and* the motorcycle scene. Of course, he didn't suggest what transpired on that bike, but that's where I come in. We're a great team. I love you, babe.

Finally, to my unique and wonderful children, who are growing up *way* too fast. To the girl—thank you for the inspiring Post-it notes you leave for me to find around the house. They keep me strong. To the boy—those amazing hugs. You, sir, give one hell of a hug. Don't ever stop.

About the Author

Abby Niles is the author of the contemporary MMA series, Love to the Extreme, and the paranormal series, The Awakening. She is also the author to the geeky romantic comedy, *Defying Convention*, where Live Action Role Players (LARPers) set out to teach their favorite author a lesson, but end up playing matchmaker instead.

Abby lives in North Carolina with the love of her life and their combined gaggle of kids. When she's not writing, she's trying to catch up on an endless pile of laundry and find time to get some much needed reading in.

Discover more Entangled Select Contemporary titles...

THE ONE THAT GOT AWAY
a *Kingston Ale House* novel by A. J. Pine

Jamie Kingston has loved his best friend Brynn Chandler for as long as he can remember, and now that he's ready to tell her, she has her sights set on someone else. Knowing this is his last chance, he asks Brynn to go on a two-week road trip. But their time alone brings old hurts to the surface, and Brynn has to decide if the one that got away lies at the end of the journey or if he's been by her side all along.

A FRIENDLY FLIRTATION
a *Friends First* novel by Christine Warner

Allison Hall is fed up with being the invisible nerdy girl. She needs confidence—and that requires a makeover and dating tips. Jared Esterly says no when his business partner and best friend Nick's little sister comes to him for advice. But when Al's attempt to make changes on her own fails spectacularly, he's there to pick up the pieces. As lessons move from the salon to the bedroom, Allison discovers change can come at a very high price.

How to Fall
a novel by Rebecca Brooks

Julia Evans puts everyone else first—but all that is about to change, starting with a spontaneous trip to Brazil. Now Julia can be anyone she wants. Like someone who's willing to have a wickedly hot hook-up with the sexy Aussie at her hotel. Except, Blake Williams may not be what he seems. Julia and Blake will have to decide if they're jumping into the biggest adventure of all or playing it safe.

Playing with Fire
a *Tangled in Texas* novel by Alison Bliss

Anna Weber is every inch the proper librarian—old-fashioned, conservatively dressed right down to her tightly clipped flaming red hair. She knows too well what it means to be burned. And she will never, *ever* fall in love–especially not with the town's red-hot fireman. But Cowboy can't resist the fiery little librarian. She'll test his patience. His control. Hell, his very *sanity*. For the first time, Cowboy's found the one fire he can't control...

Discover the **Love to the Extreme** *series…*

EXTREME LOVE

FIGHTING LOVE

WINNING LOVE

HEALING LOVE

Also by Abby Niles

THE AWAKENING: AIDAN

THE AWAKENING: LIAM

THE AWAKENING: BRITTON

CPSIA information can be obtained
at www.ICGtesting.com
Printed in the USA
BVOW08s1655181217
503103BV00001B/40/P